5to

"(Readers) will recognize that Tad's and Ronnie's problems are similar to their own. Well-told story of the problems and frustrations as well as the triumphs of growing up."—*Journal of Reading*

"Because his best friend has moved away, Tad Brokaw is having a lonely, dull summer vacation until he meets Ronnie White Cloud. The Indian boy and the white boy discover common interests and their pranks, games, and good times enliven a story of friendship."—ALA *The Booklist*

"Well-written story. Two boys share many discoveries about themselves and their ability to deal with the sometimes hostile adult world."—St. Louis *Post-Dispatch*

Dakota Sons

illustrated by Tony Chen

Dakota Sons

by Audree Distad

A HARPER TROPHY BOOK

HARPER & ROW, PUBLISHERS

New York, Evanston, San Francisco, London

DAKOTA SONS

Text copyright © 1972 by Audree Distad
Illustrations copyright © 1972 by Tony Chen

Standard Book Number: 06—440050—6

First printed in 1972.

FIRST TROPHY EDITION

For my parents

Dakota Sons

Preface

IN 1750, the Sioux, or the "Dakotahs," were the largest Indian nation along the upper Missouri River. The ancient name "Dakotah" meant "alliance with friends." But to their foes, the Chippewas, they were "Nadowe-is-iw," meaning "snakes" or "enemies." Early French explorers wrote the word as "Nadowes-sioux." Later it was shortened to "Sioux," as the Dakotahs are known today.

Although the Sioux have a common language, there are three main dialects, or special versions. The eastern Santee Sioux dialect is called Dakota; the central Yankton Sioux use Nakota; the western Teton Sioux speak Lakota.

North and South Dakota share the name of that ancient nation. There are fifteen Sioux tribes living in the Dakotas, Nebraska, and Minnesota. The largest Sioux reservations are in South Dakota.

Chapter 1

HIS best friend had moved away. Tad tossed in his bed, remembering. Bobby'd gone all the way down to Little Creek. There went the summer. No picnics, no bike rides, no sleep-outs, no nothing.

And today, he groaned, there's Clifford. I can almost hear him puffing around the school yard —most of the little kids run faster. Bobby would sure hoot if he knew I was going out to Clifford's.

Might as well get on with it, he thought. I'll have to hurry to catch the mail truck.

1

He pulled on denims, a T-shirt, and sneakers. Then he combed his stiff brown hair with his fingers. He glanced at the advertisement tucked in the corner of his mirror:

AUTHENTIC INDIAN MOCCASINS
Make Them Yourself

Kit has pre-cut leather—ready to lace, easy instructions. Your choice of beaded insignia for the toe—Sioux eagle, Cheyenne medicine arrow, Arapaho morning star.

Sure wish they'd hurry and send that kit, he thought. Wonder what the eagle looks like.

"Come on, Tad. Cereal's on the table," his mother called.

The kitchen was steamy from the washing machine, and smelled of starch. He straddled a chair and ate quickly. At least he wouldn't have to help hang out laundry. "So long, Mom." He hurried to the door.

"Dad will drive out for you after supper." And she added, "Behave yourself, now."

"Oh, Mom." He slammed the screen door behind him.

The fresh air cheered him and he liked the sound of his steps on the wooden walk leading to the street. At the corner he cut across the dusty churchyard and went diagonally through the

2

block, coming out behind the filling station. He hopscotched the oily patches of ground and waved at Mr. Hayes, the owner.

In front of the post office, Mr. McKenzie tossed a canvas mailbag into the back of the jeep.

"Hi, Mac," Tad called.

"Morning, Tad," said the paunchy mailman. "Climb in. We're about ready."

He settled a low square box of baby chicks in the back. Tad gingerly slid a finger through an air hole in the side. It was pecked and pinched before he jerked it free.

Mac laughed as he squeezed into the driver's seat. "They're little, but they're feisty. You can help me put mail in the boxes as we go," he added. They drove south past the feed store and rumbled over the train tracks at the edge of town.

Ahead, Tad saw Choco walking alone at the side of the road. The old Indian moved as though he were leading a procession. He carried a walking stick, and on his head was a high-domed black hat with a silver band.

"Bet he's going to the store," said Tad. "Sometimes he brings in eggs to trade and sometimes he just stands around for a while. I guess it's his way of visiting."

"How he raises chickens in that little shed of his beats me," said Mac. "His own house isn't

3

much bigger than a chicken coop."

"Dad says when Grandpa ran the store, Choco used to bring in beadwork to trade." Tad liked to imagine Choco as a chief, dressed in fringed leggings and a beaded shirt. But Choco didn't even wear moccasins like the ones Tad had sent away for. In the winter the old man wore a long khaki army coat with tarnished brass buttons. It made him look even taller than usual, and both majestic and forlorn.

Mac raised his arm, and Choco nodded as they passed.

"Yeah, that Choco's a tough old bird," said Mac, shaking his head. "Got a wife and four children, all buried up there on the hill. Last son came home from the army in a pine box. It would've killed most people, but not Choco."

Tad looked away to a far hill where he could see the small Indian church. Beside it was a cemetery with rows of white crosses. Some had words written in the Lakota language. On top of a child's grave Tad had once seen a tiny red truck. He still wondered who had placed it there.

They bumped along in silence. At each mailbox, Mac reached into the bag and handed Tad the mail. Tad stretched far out and shoved it into the box and slammed the tin door shut. "Okay," he said.

4

"You make my job easier," said Mac. "As a rule it's pretty dull, but one little girl left a basket of candy in the box. Course, sometimes there's a joker like Bobby Shaw. He put in a big bull snake. It hissed so it sounded just like a rattler. Scared me plenty, I'll tell you."

Tad squirmed and changed the subject. "Bobby's folks have moved to Little Creek."

Mac glanced at him. "I suppose it gets lonesome around here for you in summer."

"You can say that again. There's nobody from my class in town. Clifford lives closest and he's twelve miles out in the country. Bobby lived only four miles. I could ride my bike out there." Tad shook his head. "Boy, it's gonna be a crummy vacation."

Mac smiled sympathetically. "You can ride along with me anytime."

They were approaching a well-traveled driveway leading to a cluster of large white buildings, set back from the road.

"It looks like a ghost town in the summer," Tad said. "Do you deliver mail to the Indian school?"

"Sure. Not much for them today, though," Mac replied. "We'll leave it in the mailbox by the road. When there's too much for the box, I drive up and unload it at the schoolhouse. You're right, it is deserted this time of year," he agreed. "But when the school kids are here there's plenty going on. Ball games and races everywhere."

"On County Rally Day," Tad told him, "they won lots of prizes in the races."

The schoolchildren often walked into town to buy candy at his father's store. As they stood talking and laughing together, Tad would watch them shyly and sometimes find one of them solemnly studying him.

Then he said to Mac, "There was an Indian boy named Melvin Three Trees in our class last year. He drew real good pictures of horses. Some of the kids teased him about his name." Bobby did, he remembered. "I don't think it's fair to tease someone, do you?"

"Bound to happen, I guess," said Mac. He stopped the jeep and looked down the driveway.

Tad turned his head, too. A tire rolled down the drive and a dark-haired boy raced beside it. His arm swung in wide strokes as he slapped the tire along. Seeing the mail truck, he upset the tire into the ditch and ran toward them.

"Hello, there," called Mac, leaning across Tad to hand the mail into the boy's hands. "You want to carry the mail in again today?"

The boy grinned at Mac and waved as the jeep pulled away. Tad put his head out the open win-

dow for another glimpse of the boy. The dust swirled behind the jeep and he ducked inside again.

"Who was that boy?" he asked.

"He must be staying at the school this summer," said Mac. "Whenever he's playing on the drive, I give him the mail to deliver. He's always alone, so I guess you two have something in common. Not enough kids around in the summer."

"That's for sure," sighed Tad, leaning back. "Maybe I could get to know him."

Chapter 2

BEYOND the school were open rolling plains. Tad liked the flying sensation as the jeep burst over each small rise.

Near the road was a flat-topped butte. It stood two hundred feet tall and three times as long, towering over the prairie.

It was called Spotted Butte, same as the town. Tad could see it from the store, but from the road he could almost count the scrawny spruce trees growing on its top and the spiky yucca plants at the base.

"Why do they call yucca 'soapweed?'" Tad asked.

"The Indians once used parts of it for soap," said Mac. "It's real pretty when it blooms, with those tall spears of white flowers."

"There were Indians living all around here once," said Tad.

"Sure. There still are, you know. On that side of the road is a Sioux reservation."

Tad nodded. "But before the reservations, the Indians must have really liked it here."

The grassy slopes were green now. They would dry and bleach to a golden tan later. Tad thought of the delicate orange and purple wildflowers which bloomed low in the tall grasses. He wondered if they really did grow on unmarked graves, as the legend said.

"There's the Potts place," said Mac at last. Clifford boosted himself off the back steps and waved as they stopped at the drive.

There's Clifford, round as a butterball, thought Tad. Then he tried to smile and wave in a friendly way. "Thanks, Mac," he said.

Clifford ambled toward him, grinning. His plaid shirt was out at both elbows, and he was furiously rubbing a plant stalk against his finger.

"What's that?" Tad asked.

"My dad told me if I rubbed milkweed juice

against a wart it would go away." He grinned again. "I been doing it all morning, but the wart's still there."

"I just read a story," Tad said, "about a boy who thought a dead cat would get rid of warts. And he—"

"Oh," groaned Clifford, "I don't want to have to read a book in the summertime."

Tad grinned. Clifford didn't read even in school. He mostly looked out the window and thought about his lunch box.

"What are we going to do?" Tad asked.

"Come on. I'll show you my brother's new pickup truck. It's old, really, but Dad just bought it for him a couple days ago. Jake will be sixteen next week, and he'll get his driver's license. This fall he can take us back and forth to school."

Clifford led the way to the pickup and peered over the side into the box. "Jake's been trapping again," he said. Tad looked into the back too. A few ears of dried corn and a tangled heap of metal lay in one corner.

Stuck to one piece of metal was a small furry object. "See this?" said Clifford, pulling it loose and holding it toward Tad.

"Well, what is it?"

"It's a raccoon's foot," Clifford told him. "Second time it's happened that I know about. Jake keeps setting traps even though Dad says we don't need to. Jake just likes to see what he can catch. This here raccoon must've got caught by one foot and then chewed it off to get away."

Tad stared at the stiff stump in Clifford's hand. It had strong nails, and knots of hair matted with dried blood. "He chewed off his own foot? Does the raccoon die then?"

Clifford shook his head. "Probably not. He just has three feet. Want to have this? Maybe it's lucky, like a rabbit's foot."

"No," snapped Tad. Clifford dropped the foot into the back of the pickup.

Jake suddenly appeared at the barn door. "Get away from my pickup," he shouted.

Clifford jerked back from the truck. "We're not doing anything," he said. Then he muttered to Tad, "We better get out of here."

Clifford's lower lip drooped and he moved away without looking at Jake. Tad glanced back. Jake waited at the door, his fists on his hips, watching to be sure they followed orders. "Stay away from it, you hear?"

Tad turned to follow Clifford, who had flopped down on the back steps of the house, his chin on his hand. Tad kicked his toe against the ground, wondering what to say. "There's lots of other things to do."

12

Clifford shook his head. "Someday I'm going to tell Jake off." After a while he slowly raised himself off the step and looked around the yard.

"We could go see the barn," he said, "except Jake's down there." Tad shook his head. Once was enough.

"If the horses were here, we could go for a ride."

"That's a great idea!"

"But they're out in the pasture today."

Tad was disappointed. "I've only been on a horse once," he told Clifford. "Bobby and I always pretended our bikes were horses."

"I don't want to do that," said Clifford.

"Want to play baseball?"

"Nah. We don't even have enough to play one o'cat."

"We could just bat and take turns."

"It's kind of hot. We'd have to chase the ball all the time."

"How about kick-the-can?"

"That's no good with just two guys."

"What, then? You never want to do anything."

"You sound just like Bobby sometimes," said Clifford.

Tad shoved his hands into his pockets. I might as well have stayed home with the laundry, he thought. "Okay. Let's do whatever you want to."

13

Clifford frowned. "I found an old BB-gun in the basement last week, and I bought some BBs in town. We could shoot at cans."

Tad brightened. "That sounds like fun."

Clifford bustled into the house and soon returned with the gun and BBs. "Let's put a couple cans on the fence over there away from the house." He took the first turn and missed twice. "Lucky I got a big box of shot," he said.

Tad closed one eye and sighted carefully down the barrel, but his first shot missed. The second BB hit the post.

Clifford knocked a can off, on his next turn. As he handed the gun to Tad, they heard another roar from the barn.

"Hey!"

Jake lunged over the high sill of the barn door, slammed down his pitchfork, and stalked across the yard toward them. "Who told you you could use my gun? Gimme that gun."

He snatched the gun with one hand and shoved Clifford with the other. Clifford stumbled and fell backward onto the ground. "Don't let me catch you horning in on any more of my stuff," Jake shouted and marched toward the house.

"I found that gun way back in the basement," Clifford yelled. "I'm gonna tell Dad you knocked me down." His eyes filled with tears, and he scrambled to his feet and pitched a rock after Jake. When it fell short, Clifford stamped the ground furiously.

Tad stared after Jake. I sure wouldn't want a brother who pushed me around, he thought. Poor Clifford. I wish I'd yelled back at Jake.

For the rest of the day Clifford vetoed any running games and Tad was too awkward to help with the chores.

At supper Jake complained, "Clifford stole my gun."

"I did not. I found it," said Clifford.

"Bet you took my BBs, too."

"No I didn't." Clifford's voice rose. "They were mine."

"Tell him to leave my stuff alone."

"He pushed me down."

Mr. Potts banged down his fork and thundered, "Be quiet!"

An embarrassed silence fell over the table and Tad didn't know where to look. Beside him, Clifford sniffed from time to time.

When he finished eating, Mr. Potts leaned back in his chair and poked a toothpick into his mouth. "From now on," he announced, "Clifford can use that gun if he buys his own shot. But any more fights and I'll throw it in the cattle dam. Now, you hear?"

Clifford grinned triumphantly at Jake, who stomped out of the kitchen.

Tad almost cheered when he saw his father's black Ford turn into the driveway. He stood impatiently while his father talked to Mr. Potts about crops and weather.

Driving home, his father asked, "Have a good time?"

"It was all right. Not as much fun as playing with Bobby." He sighed. "And that Jake's a mean guy for a brother." He sat back and watched the sunset colors light up the side of Spotted Butte.

"Tomorrow you can help me at the store," his father told him.

"Sure," said Tad. "I got a whole vacation of nothing to do."

His father chuckled. "It'll be a fine summer. You'll see."

Chapter 3

AFTER breakfast the next morning, Tad and his father left the house for the store. At the corner they saw Pinto, their neighbor's dog —a large buff-colored Great Dane with red-rimmed eyes and the temper of a bronco.

"Would you look at the whopper of a bone he's got," said Tad.

"Good scavenging last night, Pinto?" His father reached out to pat the dog's head. Pinto growled. Tad walked around him.

At the gasoline station, his father nodded a greeting to Mr. Hayes.

"Morning, Jim," said Mr. Hayes. "Gonna be a hot one."

Tad blinked up at the brilliant sky. It made his eyes smart. A gust of warm wind hit his cheeks.

Beyond the station they passed the Rainbow Cafe. Tad waved at Mac, who sat inside having coffee. His empty jeep was parked next door at the post office.

Across the street stood an old bank building, which now held a dry-goods store on the main floor and a small library on the attic floor. Beside it, the barber's house had a barber shop on the front sunporch.

At the far corner was a pool hall named The Lasso. The owner was sweeping the sidewalk beneath a wide wooden canopy. Along the edge of the canopy hung a row of white cattle skulls.

His father's store was on the next corner. It had a square false front with a pitched roof behind it. Across the top a sign said GENERAL MERCANTILE, just as it had when Tad's grandfather built the store. In the corner, the sign read:

JAMES BROKAW, Prop.

"Your name is on the sign," said Tad. "Did Grandpa have his name on it, too?"

"Yes. When it was built it said Thaddeus Brokaw, Proprietor."

18

Tad felt proud remembering that name, glad it was his own full name. Sharing it made him feel close to his grandfather.

"When did Grandpa come to South Dakota?" Tad couldn't hear the story often enough.

"When he was a boy. His dad, your great-grandfather, first lived in the eastern part of the state. Then he packed up and came out here to 'west river' country."

"I'm glad he did," said Tad. "It's prettier out here, west of the Missouri. Go on."

"Your great-granddad kept his store goods in a farm wagon and went from place to place, wherever there were customers. Your grandpa rode with him in the wagon when he was your age." Tad especially liked imagining that.

"Why don't we do that? Take the goods around."

His father laughed. "That's just history now. Besides, people want some excuse to come to town." He unlocked the padlock on the front door and pushed it open.

Tad stopped outside to straighten the green wooden bench beneath the front window. Often on summer days, two or three Indian women would sit on the bench, talking in their Lakota language. Tad could hear them from inside the store, their voices moving in musical patterns,

19

none of which he understood. It was fun to listen and wonder.

Now he followed his father into the store. It felt cool inside.

"Here's a box of overalls you can put on those shelves." His father gestured toward the far wall, where shelves stretched from floor to ceiling. At one side was a stepladder.

"I'll put out the meat," said his father. He yanked open the door of the meat locker. Tad felt the chilly air hit his face. Inside he glimpsed sides of beef hanging in the icy room.

Tad slit the top of the cardboard box with a jackknife. He folded the blue-denim overalls carefully and arranged them with large sizes on the bottom and the small ones on top. The mens' went in one stack, the boys' in another.

In the next box, he found straw hats. He pulled out the first one and set it far back on his head at a jaunty angle. He curled the wide brim against the crown so it would be more like a cowboy hat.

He was trying to find his reflection in the window, to see how the hat looked, when a battered blue pickup truck stopped with a bump against the curb. Sunshine reflected like a spotlight off the windshield. Tad squinted and turned away. He recognized the pickup. It would be George Jefferson, who collected the groceries for the Indian

20

school. He grinned at the short bowlegged man as he came into the store.

"Hi, Jefferson!"

Jefferson smiled and his face wrinkled like leather. He bobbed his head at Tad. "Gotcha earning your keep, have they? Your dad here?"

Mr. Brokaw stepped from the locker. "Hello, Jefferson. Be right with you." He slid two trays of meat into the glass refrigerator counter. "Anyone at the school, now the school year's over?"

"Not many," Jefferson replied. "Few teachers finishing reports. Of course, the Burdoinnes will be there all summer. There's a couple kids with them. Joe Running Elk's working at Hayes' station and staying at the school. And there's a young kid." He handed a shopping list to Mr. Brokaw, who turned to the food shelves behind the counter.

Tad edged forward as they were talking. Now he thought of the boy with the tire. He asked in a burst, "How old is that other boy?"

"What's that?" asked Jefferson, smiling again.

"How old is the other boy at the school? You didn't say his name."

"Well, now," Jefferson began, "if you mean Ronnie White Cloud, why don't you ask him? He's right outside in the pickup."

Tad turned back to the window, peering

against the bright reflection. Sure enough, there was someone else there. Probably the boy he'd seen yesterday. What will I say, he wondered.

He hesitated at the screen door, trying not to stare toward the pickup. Awkwardly he pushed open the door and stepped down to the sidewalk. He wondered if the boy had seen him. He still couldn't think of anything to say. Aiming to be casual, he ambled to the end of the bench and sat down and looked away down the street. From the corner of his eye he could see the boy's face—slender and almond-shaped.

The boy had one sturdy arm propped on the open window frame and his chin rested on it. He was looking down at the fender where a butterfly fanned its wings. All the while Tad felt the boy was secretly watching him too.

He is about my age, Tad told himself. If he'd look up, maybe I could say something. What? What could I say? Tad studied the street again as a Russian thistle bounced along in the breeze. Now or never, he decided. "Hi," he volunteered.

Slowly the boy turned his brown eyes on Tad. "Hi," he answered.

They each glanced away, as if embarrassed. From inside the store Tad heard the voices of his father and Jefferson. He's coming to the door, Tad thought. Are they leaving already? In his confusion he jumped up, still tongue-tied. The boy looked curiously at him, but Tad only blinked back.

"Much obliged," said Jefferson at the door.

"Sure thing," answered Mr. Brokaw. He held the screen door open for Jefferson, who carried a box of groceries.

Jefferson hoisted the groceries into the back and settled them on the floor of the pickup. "So you met Ronnie," he said to Tad. "I suppose you two been chewing the fat some." He chuckled. "Sorry to go so soon, but we gotta get this food back."

He stepped up into the pickup cab, ground the gears into action, and Tad watched them jolt away down the street. He almost shouted, "Hey, wait a minute." But he walked sheepishly back into the store.

While he finished stacking the hats on a shelf, he lectured himself. I could have said, "It's gonna be a hot one." He ripped open a carton filled with denim shirts. Could have said, "Saw you yesterday from the mail truck." He slapped the shirts onto a shelf with the sizes helter-skelter. Or I could have asked him if he had a bicycle.

Now there! It's not far out to the school, he thought. Three miles? A bike could make that easy.

He turned toward the counter. "Maybe I'll ride my bike out to the country this afternoon."

His father, prying at a wooden crate of fresh fruit, only muttered, "Fine, fine."

"Maybe I'll stop by the Indian school and see what that boy is doing."

The crate opened with a crack. His father laid down the claw hammer he was using. He looked around. "What boy?"

"Ronnie White Cloud," said Tad impatiently. "At the school."

"Oh," said his father. "All right. I'm sure Prof Burdoinne won't mind." He gestured toward the back storeroom. "There are some more boxes out there. Think you can carry them in here yourself?"

"You bet," said Tad. If I finish here by noon, he thought, I can ride out early.

Chapter 4

TAD gulped his sandwich that noon and hurried outside to his bicycle.

The road leading out of town had a slight downgrade, followed by a steep hill. He wanted to make the hill without stopping. He leaned forward over the handlebars, pedaling to a high speed which carried him partway up the steep section. Gradually the strokes became stiffer. Each one was a separate effort. His knees ached until they felt hot. Just below the rise, they knotted. He stopped, rested his shaking legs, then pushed the bicycle to the hilltop.

There he looked back at the town. It was his favorite lookout. Tad liked the way the town was framed at one end by two grain elevators and at the other by the church spire.

He could see his father's store clearly. At the edge of town was an old red depot, and opposite it was Choco's house. The railroad track ran between them. Tad knew the track bed was almost overgrown with weeds, since the train came through only once a week.

He stood, feeling lazy in the summer sun, breathing in the sweet scent of the wild yellow clover in the ditch. Then he climbed onto his bike and headed toward the school.

He tried not to think about actually meeting the new boy. He wondered again what he should say. Bobby and Clifford, he'd known them even before they started school together. And he knew nearly everybody who came into the store. But he couldn't remember ever going out to meet someone he didn't know at all.

Another mile and he was at the driveway. Across the open field, the buildings seemed to be watching him. He guessed that the white stucco building, two stories high, was for classes. In front of it a flag fluttered, the metal pulley clanking against the pole.

Clustered near the school were smaller buildings, and behind them was the arched top of a gymnasium. The team's symbol, a coyote, was painted high across the front. But he did not see anyone moving about.

Now that Tad was so close, he hesitated. Maybe I ought to ride home again, he thought. I don't even know where to look.

What would Bobby say, he wondered, if he could see me here. Then he frowned. He'll be making new friends too. I know he will, even though he said he's my best friend.

He heard a hollow sound. *Thunk.* It seemed to come from behind the school. It sounded again. He took a deep breath and guided the bike around the corner.

There he found a playground, empty except for a slim boy in blue jeans and a striped shirt, playing basketball. *Thunk,* the ball hit the rim. The boy caught the rebound with one hand and pivoted. Seeing Tad, he stopped short. They stared in surprise at each other.

"Hi," blurted Tad.

The boy straightened and looked directly at Tad. "Hi," he said.

Tad felt like an intruder before this solemn boy. "I saw you in town." His own voice sounded squeaky to him. "My name is Tad."

The boy shifted the ball into the crook of his

28

arm. Straight dark hair flopped partly over his forehead. He had a long narrow nose and a gentle mouth. "Mine's Ronnie."

The boy wasn't smiling, but he didn't seem unfriendly either. Tad eased the bicycle to the ground. "Jefferson said you were going to be around this summer. I thought maybe you'd like someone to play with." He waited.

Ronnie nodded slowly. "I guess," he said. "Do you play basketball?"

"Sure," said Tad, feeling better. "I've got a basket on our shed. Not as high as this one though." He looked doubtfully at the bare hoop and the backboard fixed on a tall pole.

"The high-school guys use this one," said Ronnie proudly. He fired off a straight shot from the chest. It bounded off the backboard, hit the rim, and bounced off. Ronnie made a face. "You try it."

Even the basketball seemed larger than usual to Tad. He sighted over the top, bent his knees and sprang up as he shot. *Thunk*, the ball rebounded from the rim. At least it got there, he thought. He passed the ball to Ronnie.

"You know Joe Running Elk?" said Ronnie.

"I saw him play basketball twice last year," said Tad. "I went to all the Friday night games. Sometimes even to the Tuesday night games." He hoped that would make him seem older.

"Joe's teaching me how to shoot," said Ronnie. "He's on the first string. High-point man last year."

"He sure can dribble too," said Tad.

"You bet. I'm gonna learn to dribble a ball like that." Ronnie bounced the ball rapidly with one hand to demonstrate. "Joe's staying here this summer," he added.

Tad pushed his head up to be as tall as possible. "What grade are you?"

"I'll be in fifth next year."

"Me, too!" Tad beamed.

"I should be in sixth," said Ronnie. "But I didn't go to school one year."

"No kidding? I thought everybody had to go to school."

Ronnie idly shot the ball. It dropped through the hoop. "Nope," he said.

They took several shots in silence. One of Tad's teetered on the hoop and rolled in.

"Whew," he sighed. "I finally made one." Ronnie grinned.

A window opened above them. Tad recognized Mr. Burdoinne, the principal of the school. His thin dark hair lay straight back above his forehead and he wore rimless glasses. "How's the game going?" He smiled at them.

"Okay," said Ronnie.

"Did you ride your bicycle out from town?" Mr. Burdoinne asked Tad. "That's a good trip."

Tad shrugged. "It's not far. I like to ride."

"You're Jim Brokaw's boy, aren't you?"

Tad nodded.

Mr. Burdoinne smiled again. "Ronnie's always glad to have another basketball player. Say hello to your dad for me." He looked at Ronnie. "How's that book coming? Is it interesting?"

Ronnie juggled the basketball lightly. "I like it," he said. Tad wouldn't have guessed so from his tone.

Mr. Burdoinne closed the window. The boys glanced at each other as if they'd been caught whispering in class. They darted out of sight around the building and burst into giggles.

"He was plenty curious," said Ronnie.

"I know," said Tad. "What did he mean about a book?"

"Now who's curious?" Ronnie teased. But his grin disappeared. "It's all about the Sioux and what they used to be. You've never read it."

"It sounds good," Tad began.

Ronnie turned away. "Can I ride your bike?"

Tad wanted to ask more questions, but instead answered, "Sure. Have you got one?"

"No, but I can ride. I learned at my last school."

31

Ronnie wheeled off down the driveway. He rides well, Tad thought. Bet he could make that hill easy. I wonder why he was so touchy about the book.

At the road, Ronnie turned the bike and pedaled slowly back. He stopped and grinned. "We played a trick on one fellow last year. He had an old bike, and on Halloween we put it up in a tree. He looked and looked for that bike. We were rolling on the ground laughing while he looked. We had to help him get it down."

"That couldn't have been around here," said Tad. "There's not a tree between here and the river."

"Nope," said Ronnie. "It was in Nebraska."

"Do you live there? Is that where you go to school?"

"We lived there awhile," Ronnie sighed. "Mr. Burdoinne is after my dad to have me stay here." He shook his head. "They went to high school together once and he's always putting his two cents in. That's why I'm here this summer."

"Is your dad a teacher, too?"

Ronnie's eyes widened. "Heck, no." He smiled mischievously. "He's a rodeo rider."

Tad gasped. "Boy, I don't know anyone else whose dad is a rodeo rider. Wow, what's he do?"

"He rides broncs," said Ronnie. "Most times I

go with him. We go all over. Won't be long till he comes to get me." He stared wistfully at the road. "I can't wait to see him."

"You mean you won't be here all summer?"

Ronnie shook his head, but he looked as though he was thinking of something else.

Tad felt disappointed. "Anyway," he said, "we could have some swell fun before you go. How about a picnic at the river? It's just a couple miles farther down the road. My mom will fix us some sandwiches. You want to?"

"Sure, when?"

"Tomorrow?"

Ronnie nodded in agreement and it was settled.

"Want to play some more basketball?"

"You bet!"

They shot baskets, taking turns, shouting and laughing, until they both were covered with dust and sweat. At last Tad wiped his dirt-streaked hands on the seat of his pants and said he had to go home.

"See you tomorrow," he promised, "about noon."

He pedaled down the drive, and at the road turned to wave. Ronnie made a high sweeping motion with his arm and turned to fire off a final basket.

Tad rode slowly on the way home, making the

ride last. Good thing I biked out, he told himself. Three miles is nothing when you have a friend to do things with. Imagine finding someone living so close to town. He's as much fun as Bobby.

The thought was out before he knew it and it amazed him. I shouldn't put one against the other that way. Well, he's more fun than Clifford. I wonder how long he'll be here?

Chapter 5

"THANKS for the lunch, Mom. I'll be careful," he said, hoping to avoid her usual reminder.

"Be careful now," she said. "Why you have to go all the way to the river, I don't know. Can't you have your picnic in the backyard?"

"I said I'd be careful!" Tad jammed the bag lunch into the bicycle basket. It was bad enough at breakfast, he thought, when she asked all about Ronnie. Lucky thing Dad was there. What did she mean, "We really don't know him"? Doesn't she want me to have any fun this summer?

Tad's annoyance lasted to the top of the steep hill. He stopped to look back at the town and the rolling fields around him and felt better. Then he rode slowly on.

Ronnie was leaning against a corner post at the end of the driveway.

"Hi," called Tad.

"Hi. You got the lunch?"

"Sure. Hop on. We'll take turns." Ronnie straddled the bicycle carrier and they wobbled off down the road.

"Boy, the balance is all off with someone on the back," puffed Tad. The handlebars twisted, and the pumping seemed as stiff as riding uphill. Tad struggled, zigzagging along the road.

Behind him, Ronnie laughed. "Let me ride you." They changed places and Ronnie handled the bike easily.

After a mile the road forked. "That's the way to Little Creek," said Tad pointing to the wide section. "This goes to the river." They turned onto a rutted path. Ahead, they could see trees growing along the river banks. A few blossoms still clung to the plum trees.

Tad thought of Mary Two Moons, who came to their kitchen door selling baskets of wild fruit each fall. "My mom makes jelly from the plums and chokecherries," he said. "It's sure good."

"Suppose she put any in the sandwiches?" Ronnie asked. "I'm hungry."

They pushed the bike along a footpath to the river. Tad took out the sandwiches wrapped in wax paper. "They're salami. Want one?"

They sat, leaning against the rough trunk of a large cottonwood tree, where they could watch the river as they ate. Shallow, clear water ran quietly over a smooth bed of sand.

"The river is full now," said Tad. "By fall sometimes there's not half this much water. You can jump across in some places."

"Let's go swimming," said Ronnie.

Tad knew what his mother would think of that idea. "It's not deep enough to swim in."

"That's all right. I can't really swim. We could just splash around."

"I guess so," Tad agreed slowly. "We could wade. You know there are some little patches of quicksand in this river. Not very deep ones, but you can sink to your knees before you hit bottom."

"No kidding. Suppose we can find one?" Ronnie began pulling off his shoes and socks and Tad followed. They rolled their Levi's above their knees.

"It's cool," said Ronnie, standing ankle-deep. "Where's the quicksand?"

"I remember there was a patch of it around

37

here last summer." Tad looked downstream. "It might be over by that big tree." He waded across. Each step left a tiny roil of sand on the bottom.

In the shade of the tree there was a dark pool undisturbed by the current. Tad grabbed an elbow of root poking through the bank and stepped into the dark water. He felt the cool sand sliding under his feet, giving way. It oozed around and over his feet and rose to hide his ankles. "This is the spot," he said without taking his eyes off the sand.

Silently, Ronnie and Tad watched the water and sand climb higher on Tad's legs. He tightened his hold on the root, and his hand hurt. The rolled pants-legs were getting wet now. Tad took a quick breath. He thought he remembered how deep it had been last summer.

Sand slipped up until it reached his knees. His pants were wet to the waist. "I'm slowing up," he said. "It's sort of a bottom." He grinned now, easing his hand on the root. "I won't sink any more." He wriggled his body from side to side to sink an inch deeper.

"Let me try it," said Ronnie.

"Give me a hand and help me out." Tad gripped Ronnie's hand, lifted one leg, and stepped toward the current. The sand sucked shut behind him. "Go ahead."

Ronnie experimented, making futile walking

motions as his feet sank. Then, he stood astride, hands on hips, as the water rose just to his finger-tips. He grinned. "Are there any really deep ones? Ones without bottoms?"

"I've heard so, but I don't know. Let's walk up-stream."

They waded around a small bend. "Look, there's a bridge ahead," said Ronnie. He ran forward to stand beneath it.

"Barely room for one car," said Tad looking up. Sunlight showed through the holes in the cross boards. "The road we followed down here must jog around this way and lead onto the bridge."

Ronnie moved forward. "There's a house here."

Tad followed him toward the bank. More like a shack, he thought, looking at a deserted green trailer-house. Its sides were chipped and freckled with rust. Pieces of torn plastic flapped at the tiny high windows. The bottom was partially covered with tar paper, and Tad could see that the trailer was propped unevenly on cement blocks.

"Looks empty," said Ronnie. "Let's go inside."

"What if someone owns it? They wouldn't like it."

"Oh, come on." Ronnie shoved the door. It lurched open and stuck against the floor. "See, it's empty." He moved inside.

Tad stepped high to clear the doorsill. Squint-

ing, he saw some old bedsprings at the far end, and a small table with an orange-crate seat beside it. Part of a stovepipe lay in one corner, and another stubby portion disappeared through the ceiling. "Smells like a cellar," he said.

Ronnie bounced on the creaking springs and set off an explosion of dust, which made him sneeze.

"Some house," said Tad. He sat on the edge of the crate.

"It's not bad, for something we just found," said Ronnie. "I know people with places like this. Lots of them." His voice was flat and final.

Tad suddenly wondered if Ronnie had lived in one. He glanced around with a slight shudder and knew he wouldn't want to. "It'd be a good club-house."

"What kind of clubhouse?"

"I don't know. We'd have to make up a club." Tad put his chin on his fists to think. "Some kind of secret club."

"How about being Contraries?" Ronnie asked.

Tad repeated the word. "What are you talking about?"

"I read about them in Mr. Burdoinne's book," Ronnie said. "They were old, courageous Sioux warriors, but only the ones who had had dreams of thunder. It was a special society, and that's

41

sort of like a club. What it meant was that they had to do everything opposite. They said 'no' when they meant 'yes,' walked backward or on their hands, shook and shivered when it was hot, rode horseback facing the tail!"

"Oh, boy, yes!" Tad was delighted. "That's a swell club. Did they have any secret signs or anything?"

Ronnie frowned. "I don't remember any, but I'll read it again. Mostly, they cheered up everyone in the village, like clowns."

Tad tapped a toe thoughtfully. "It's a terrible day, isn't it?"

Ronnie looked up, puzzled. Then, he grinned. "It's so cold!" They laughed.

"Are you still hungry?" asked Ronnie.

"Definitely, no," said Tad. "Let's don't go back to the bicycle."

"I don't agree," said Ronnie, backing toward the door.

Tad tugged it shut after them and they slipped and slid down the bank to the river. Giggling, they inched backward, downstream. "We must never come on another picnic," said Tad.

"No fun at all," Ronnie answered. Then he stopped and gave a low whistle. "Look."

A few feet away, head high above the surface,

a brown snake was floating downstream.

Tad flinched, ready to run, but Ronnie stayed still. So Tad set his feet and waited. They watched the current carry the snake closer and then past them, moving on silently around the bend.

"We could almost reach out and touch him," said Ronnie.

Tad shuddered. "Too close. Wonder what kind it was."

"Some old water snake. Say, you shy of water snakes?"

"No, I'm not," snapped Tad.

"That means you are," Ronnie singsonged. "Fraid of a little snake."

"I am not!" Tad stalked away, rounding the bend with wary glances in all directions. Snake's gone, he thought. Ronnie's not going to call *me* a sissy.

Just then something slid along the bare back of his leg. Something firmer than the current. And slithery.

He yelped and thrashed ahead, with the river dragging around his ankles. The sand slipped underfoot and he pitched forward in the water. Spluttering, coughing, he heard a howl behind him.

Ronnie had one hand clapped over his mouth,

muffling his laughter. His right hand held a wet green twig. He wagged it. "Want a snake?"

"It's not funny," shouted Tad. He crept to his feet, rubbing one knee. His sopping shirt was chilly on his chest.

"You really jumped," said Ronnie. "Clear out of the water. You could have won a broad jump." He grinned widely.

Tad pushed his wet hair off his face and waded to shore. Ronnie followed, grinning, trying not to laugh out loud.

Tad peeled off the wet T-shirt and hung it over the bicycle basket to dry. Water ran off his blue jeans and drizzled down inside, along his legs.

They rummaged through the sack for cookies and apples, and ate standing up. The ground was warm underfoot and Tad's jeans dried in the sunshine. Beside him, Ronnie yawned and stretched. They grinned at each other.

Tad sighed. "I guess it's time to head home." He offered the last cookie to Ronnie, who crumbled it and sprinkled the crumbs near an ant hill. They watched the ants discover this feast and dart about, tugging it home.

Then they pushed the bike between them toward the main road.

"Tell me some more about that book," said Tad. "About the Sioux."

Ronnie frowned. "Well, it said they hunted buffalo," he began, "and the herds were so big, they looked like brown oceans."

"Yeah, we read that in school," said Tad. He looked across the empty plains, trying to imagine a brown, trudging ocean. "I sure would like to have seen that.

"Once I saw some pictures in a magazine," he told Ronnie, "and they had been taken right around here. They called the Sioux 'unemployed buffalo hunters.' "

To Tad's surprise, Ronnie threw back his head with a whoop of laughter. "Wait till I tell my dad," he hooted. "He wondered why he couldn't get a job!" And he burst out laughing again.

Tad felt as though he'd just blurted out that two and two made five. "But he has got a job," Tad said, "with the rodeo."

Ronnie looked at him and said, "Hey, I'm not laughing at you. I mean, I know *you* didn't say that. It just struck me so funny."

Ronnie was quiet again as he walked on. "My dad's not always in rodeos. He works for road crews, too. Lots of times." He looked away.

"I'll bet you like it best when he's in a rodeo, though," said Tad.

Ronnie was silent for a moment. "Yeah," he said, as if he'd lost an argument.

Tad tried to remember how they'd gotten into the rodeo talk. He said, "I also read that when the Sioux hunted food, they shared it all equally. They shared everything together."

"You sure read a lot."

"I like to," said Tad. "I like to imagine how things were, right here, everywhere we look. Besides, the chiefs seem so noble and—" He stopped short as Ronnie's face changed from thoughtful to sad. Now what did I say wrong? Tad wondered.

"Maybe that's how they were," Ronnie replied slowly. "It doesn't make much difference now." He was quiet, as though he didn't know an answer. "I've never really lived on a reservation, except for a few weeks or so. My dad moves around. He says a reservation is just a place to be away from. He never talks much about . . . about being an Indian."

Ronnie kicked a stone that went skittering ahead of them. "Usually I go to town schools, and whenever something comes up about Indians, everyone watches me. Maybe they're trying to see if I'm noble or something. But I think they just don't like me."

Tad wished he could drop out of sight. He kept thinking of Melvin Three Trees and how Bobby had teased him. It seemed worse the more he thought about it, remembering that Melvin would shrug and walk away. I didn't know how he was feeling inside, Tad thought.

"You're not like those kids," Ronnie said quietly. "You're different."

Not much different, Tad thought, turning away. I should have told Bobby to shut up, he decided. Next time I will, too. I'm sure I will. I've never talked with an Indian about Indians before. I figured the past would be pretty interesting to Ronnie, but he doesn't seem to want any part of it. Bet he'd laugh if he knew I'd ordered that moccasin kit.

"You and Mr. Burdoinne'd make some pair," Ronnie said to him. "He'd keep you reading all summer and then some." He shook his head in wonder. "I asked him a question last week and he talked for an hour. All I wanted was to get outside and shoot baskets."

Tad grinned. "That sounds like a teacher all right."

"But the worst part is . . ." Ronnie began and then stopped.

"What?"

The way Ronnie sighed, Tad knew he'd been brooding about something.

"Mr. Burdoinne has taken it into his head to

47

teach me an old Indian dance. He wants me to dance at a powwow down at Santee. And I'm not about to!"

Tad started to say that it sounded like fun, but instead he nodded in sympathy, still puzzled.

"My dad says the dances don't mean anything anymore," Ronnie went on. "So why should I learn them?"

Tad didn't know how to answer him. Ronnie seemed caught up in his own thoughts as they walked on.

At the main road, Ronnie motioned Tad onto the bicycle carrier and he pedaled as they rode toward home. Tad wished the afternoon were just beginning. This is how I hoped summer would be, he thought. I'm glad Ronnie's around.

"Ronnie, could you come and stay overnight at my place sometime? My friend Bobby used to do that."

"Maybe, if it's before my dad comes."

He's sure set on leaving, Tad thought. It must be strange, not having your own folks around. I guess I'd feel that way too.

At the school driveway, they parted.

"It was an awful picnic," Ronnie began.

"How wrong you are," answered Tad, nodding his head. "And I hope I don't see you again too soon."

Ronnie slowly backed toward the school, shouting, "Hello, hello!"

Tad swung around on his bicycle seat and grabbed the handlebars behind him. With one foot toeing the ground for balance, he wobbled off backward down the road.

Chapter 6

A LONG silver truck rumbled into town with its weekly delivery. Tad watched the driver jockey the carrier up to the back door of the store. One by one, cartons of new stock were unloaded and toted into the back room.

Tad and his mother unpacked and arranged some of the goods, while his father helped with the unloading. The largest box they opened contained bolts of material. His mother pushed the stepladder up to the shelf marked Yard Goods and Notions.

"Hand me those bolts, can you, Tad?" She

stretched her arms down toward him. "Are they too heavy?"

"No, no. I can do it." He bent over the box, lifted one, and nearly dropped it. It felt as heavy as his whole bicycle. He flexed his arms, bent, and slowly lifted bolts up, one at a time. They must weigh more at the bottom, he thought, dragging up another.

"Isn't this a nice print," said his mother studying the material Tad held up.

"For Pete's sake, Mom, will you hurry!" His arms ached from holding the bolt. At least, he thought, it's the last one. This may be a good time to ask. "Mom?"

"Yes? That's all the material?"

"That's all." He straightened his shoulders and cleared his throat. "Mom, can Ronnie stay overnight?"

"Ronnie?" She looked surprised. "You mean the boy from the Indian school?"

"Yes. We had a swell time on our picnic."

"Well, I don't know," his mother began. She examined the label on a box of thread as if she were reading the small print. Finally, she sighed. "We'll see."

"But, Mom, I thought maybe he could come tonight. You always let Bobby stay." Tad's voice rose as he spoke. She turned away. "We

51

won't be any trouble, honest."

Her soft voice clipped each word. "I said 'We'll see.' " Her hands slapped the small boxes into place on the shelf. Then she added, "We'll ask your father."

"Ask me what?" Tad's father had come up behind them and put a large carton on the counter. He smiled and looked from one to the other. "Ask me what?"

"I want Ronnie to stay overnight."

Mr. Brokaw glanced quickly at his wife. His smile stiffened. "I don't see why Tad shouldn't have a friend over," he said solemnly.

"But, Jim," she said, "we don't know him." She looked nervously at Tad. "Maybe the school wouldn't let him come."

"Oh, I don't know why not," said Mr. Brokaw. "As long as they know where he is. I'll call Prof Burdoinne and ask him."

His mother raised her chin. "If you both are agreed, then that's that."

"It'll be all right, Mom. You'll see." Tad didn't remember ever defending a friend before. "You'll like Ronnie."

Mr. Brokaw returned from telephoning at the far end of the store. "Ronnie will walk into town in a little while."

"That's swell," said Tad. "Can we sleep in the

backyard? We could make a tent."

His father laughed, and even his mother smiled at his plan. "The pioneer," said Mr. Brokaw.

"You can roast wieners outside if you like," his mother added.

"I can't wait!" Tad looked at the big pendulum clock hanging behind the meat counter. Four o'clock. "Do you need any more help?" He suddenly had an errand. "I want to go to the library. I have to get a book before tonight."

His mother laughed and shook her head. "Go, so I can get some work done," she said.

He raced toward the dry-goods store in the next block. It was owned by Mrs. Dexter, a gnarled, peppery woman who seemed to be as old as the town. Her wiry gray hair was wound in a loose bun on top her head.

Her store had the only toy counter in town, and on Saturday evenings the youngsters gathered there to paw through the toys. "Get out, get out," she would cry. "Where are your folks? Don't they ever watch you?"

To reach the library Tad had to walk through her store. He closed the door carefully behind him. "Hello, Mrs. Dexter." She complained to his mother if he wasn't polite. "Is the library open?"

She peered over the top of the newspaper she was reading behind the counter. "Afternoon, Tad.

Can't say that it is. You're the only person to come today." She rose uncertainly. "Now where's that key?" She opened the cash register and poked through the coins.

"You're the steadiest customer," she added. "Going to read more Laura Ingalls Wilder books, I'll bet." She slammed the cash drawer, frowned, and rummaged through a basket of papers. "Here's the key," she said at last. "You lock up after yourself before you come down. I don't want to have to climb those stairs. And don't forget to turn off the light after you."

Tad ran up the stairs and unlocked the library door at the top. The air was hot and thick. He waved his hand through the dimness to find the light cord overhead. Bookcases, half full of books, stood forlornly against the walls.

He dragged a chair close to the children's bookshelves and read through the titles, looking for just the right book, wishing he could read them all. On the last shelf he found what he wanted.

He clattered downstairs and handed Mrs. Dexter the key and the book. She removed the card and carefully wrote his name on it. Tad wished she would hurry.

Finally, she closed the book, held it up, and squinted at the title. "*Indian Sign Language*," she read in surprise. "With all those other books upstairs, why did you pick this one?"

"I like reading about the Indians," said Tad. He reached for the book, but Mrs. Dexter was holding it to the light for a better look. Tad knew that when she started to talk she would go on and on —she probably hadn't talked to anyone all day.

"Bad enough, having those Indians around," she said. "They don't come in here much, I can tell you."

"But lots of Indians buy from my dad," said Tad. He kept his eyes on the book, waiting for a chance. "And there are lots of nice kids at the school."

"That school!" She slammed the book onto the counter. "I never did know why they built that school right outside town."

Tad figured he didn't want to hear any more, but he squared his shoulders. "I have a friend at that school. And he's coming to stay with me tonight." He stopped and took a breath. "We're going to read that book." Maybe she'd change her mind if she knew that.

Mrs. Dexter's mouth fell open. She slapped her other hand on the counter top and strained forward. "Staying overnight! What's your mother thinking of?"

Tad jerked back as if he'd been slapped. Without thinking, he shouted. "Gimme my book!" He darted forward and yanked the book from under her hand. The move upset her balance and her elbow whacked the register.

She glared at him. "Wait until I see your mother. I'll tell her what I think of Indians!"

Tad booted open the screen door and slammed it so hard the spring hammered against the frame.

He ran with the book clenched in his hand. She doesn't even know Ronnie, he thought. She's a dumb old lady. He jogged to a stop and angrily kicked a sharp rock. That's for you, old lady.

But he couldn't kick away the sad feeling. I wish I hadn't even gone over there, he thought. At least Ronnie hadn't heard her—that was something. Then he hurried so he would be home before Ronnie arrived.

Chapter 7

"A TENT! I never slept in a tent," said Ronnie.

"Well, if you're scared . . ." Tad hinted.

Ronnie pretended to be furious. "No!" They laughed together.

"Come on. Let's get the blankets. We'll pin them over the clothesline." Tad held them while Ronnie clipped the tops to the line.

"We could pound sticks at the corners to hold the sides out," Ronnie suggested.

"I don't think Mom wants holes in the blankets. Maybe rocks will work." They settled on two rocks, a can filled with nails, and a crowbar. Tad spread a thick, tufted comforter over the ground. They crawled inside and stretched out.

Ronnie lay on his back, hands folded under his head. "This is a nice tent," he said. "It could be our clubhouse if we didn't already have one."

"What'd you do all day?" Tad asked.

"Shot some baskets," said Ronnie. "And then," he made a face, "the Burdoinnes had me plant a garden. Boy, I've been shoveling and hoeing and everything. I was sure glad when your dad called."

"What did you plant?"

"Oh, potatoes and beans and zinnias."

"Zinnias! They're flowers. You can't eat zinnias."

"I know," said Ronnie impatiently. "But I found the seeds in the storeroom," he grinned, "and I thought how surprised Mr. Burdoinne will be when flowers come up."

"He'll take one look and think he needs new glasses," said Tad.

"Anyone home?" a voice called.

"We're here, Mom," said Tad, crawling out of the tent. "This is Ronnie."

"Hello, Ronnie." She looked directly into his face.

Ronnie met her eyes shyly and spoke very softly. "Hello."

Tad watched his mother's face anxiously. When she smiled at Ronnie, Tad beamed.

"Looks as though you boys have been busy," she said. "That's quite a tent." She ducked her head to peek inside. "When you get hungry, let me know." She smiled again and went into the house.

Ronnie watched her solemnly, every step of the way. "I'm glad we didn't poke holes in the blankets," he said at last. He turned somber eyes toward Tad. "My mother died."

That's why he's extra anxious to see his dad, Tad thought. Awkwardly, he said, "I'm sorry."

Ronnie stooped and entered the tent. "If it weren't for my dad, I'd have to live at a school all the time. Boy, I wouldn't like that."

Tad tried to think of something else to talk about. Then he remembered. "I have a book for us, for our club." He ran to the back door, where he had left the book, and came back to the tent with it. "It's about sign language."

Ronnie flipped the pages. "Here's 'friend,'" he said. He held up his left hand, palm out, in the ancient salute. "Left hand because it's nearer the heart," he read. Tad imitated the sign.

"Me," said Ronnie, jerking his right thumb toward himself. "You," he continued, pointing the thumb at Tad.

"You, friend," said Tad making both gestures. He hoped Ronnie would repeat those signs, but Ronnie was studying the motions for "night" and "sunrise."

From the kitchen window, Mrs. Brokaw watched their silent pantomime and chuckled to herself. Some time later they came in and stood before her. Each one gave the sign for "me." Then they dropped their hands to stomach level, palms up, and jerked them back and forth.

"Hmmmm," she said. "Don't tell me, let me guess what you want. I'm sure you're not hungry yet. Must be something else."

Tad and Ronnie burst into laughter.

His father stacked some kindling for the campfire in front of the tent. After eating roasted wieners with potato chips, they got the book and looked up the sign for campfire. The spreading twilight made reading impossible, and soon it was even too dark for a game of catch.

"We can watch the embers. I like that," said Tad. He stretched out in the tent to watch the dying fire. Resting his head on his arm, he could smell smoke on his skin.

Gradually their whispers faded, along with the fire, and Ronnie seemed to be asleep. Tad struggled with a weed which poked his back through the quilt. He was tossing to get comfortable when he heard a low reedy sound. Abruptly, he sat up. "Ronnie," he whispered, "are you asleep?"

"Not the way you've been jumping around," muttered Ronnie.

"Listen. Hear that whistle?"

"What is it?"

"It's the train. Comes in once a week, Monday night at eleven. It stays about twenty minutes and leaves. Want to go see it?"

Ronnie laughed. "How could we do that?"

"Be quiet. Follow me." Tad looked toward the house and listened. There were no lights. He decided his parents must be asleep. Slowly, he crept out of the tent, followed by Ronnie.

They crouched and tiptoed toward the alley. Then they ran lightly to the street. In the darkness ringing the circle of street light, they paused. The whistle sounded again, nearer now.

"Hurry," said Tad. They sprinted down the street to the railroad station. "This way," he said, motioning Ronnie away from the platform. "We don't want the station agent to see us."

"Why not?"

"He might tell my dad. And Dad wouldn't like me running around town so late. Have you got a penny?"

"Yeah, why?"

"Come on. I'll show you." He darted to the

61

tracks. The light of the train was clear and growing steadily larger. The whistle blasted through the air. "Put your penny on the track!"

They dived back to the ditch and watched the huge engine charge past. Sparks shot from the wheels, spangling the air above them. They cupped their hands over their ears to muffle the noise. Behind the engine were two freight cars, a flatcar, and a caboose. The train screeched for a few seconds, then stopped in a wheeze just beyond the station.

Tad waved Ronnie forward. "Let's find our pennies."

Ronnie was first. "Look, this must be it. It's wavy and funny-shaped."

"Here's mine," said Tad. "It's an oval." They turned the coins over and over, comparing them.

"Suppose these pennies are lucky pieces now?" asked Ronnie.

"I don't know," Tad answered. "We'll have to wait and see." He was looking down at his, squinting in the dim light from the station, when a string of loud bangs made him jump and nearly drop the penny. He and Ronnie stared at each other, puzzled.

Before either one could speak, there was a second series of cracks and shots, lasting even longer than the first. This time, Ronnie pointed

toward the direction of the sound.

"I saw flashes over there," he said.

Tad's eyes followed in the direction Ronnie gestured. "Old Choco lives that way," he told Ronnie. "What do you think it could be?"

Crack, crack, crack. The reports came again, but this time there was another volley of noises, too, on a lower note. Tad thought he saw a car parked beside the ditch. A house was visible where a dim edge of light showed around a window shade.

"It is Choco's house," he exclaimed. "But the sound isn't at the house exactly. It's off to the side." Now another noise added to the confusion: the sound of furious flapping and squawking.

While the boys watched they saw more small explosive flashes and heard the same low, peppering pops and a frenzy of clucking.

"Sounds like firecrackers!" said Tad.

"Or BBs," added Ronnie, "or maybe both. Is there a chicken coop over there?"

"Yes," said Tad, trying to picture the area in memory. "Choco has chickens, I know."

Suddenly a rectangle of light spilled through a doorway and silhouetted a figure, tall and erect, leaning lightly against a cane.

"That's Choco," breathed Tad, as the figure

moved silently out into the darkness. At once he wanted to shout, "Go back, go back."

Now several shadowy forms raced back and forth across the patch of light. They were whooping the way attacking Indians did in the movies Tad had seen. A few more single bangs, and then the sound of an engine revving up. Headlights flashed on and Tad could see a pickup truck, which sped away down the road and headed out of town. It was followed by the sound of metal dragging and clanking across the gravel.

Choco was moving slowly about the dark yard, shooing the frightened chickens back toward their coop.

"We ought to help him," Ronnie said.

"I guess so," said Tad without moving. "Except I don't want my folks to know we were here so late."

"Well, I don't care. I'm going to help." Ronnie scrambled down the bank of the railroad track. "Wait for me." He ran toward the cabin light.

Tad watched him go with growing confusion. He's right, Tad thought. Why didn't I go to help too? Angry with himself, he slumped down and dropped his chin against his knees.

My folks would be angry, he told himself again, if they knew we sneaked off. But, he argued, they might not find out. He looked toward the cabin. Choco entered and closed the door behind him.

It was quieter now—only an occasional muffled cluck carried through the air. Then Ronnie was coming and Tad stood up to join him on the street.

"Get all the chickens back in the coop?"

"Yeah, I guess," said Ronnie. "I couldn't see very well." His voice was slow and sad. "The old man was surprised to see me helping. Maybe he thought one of those guys was still there."

"Who were they?"

Ronnie shrugged. "I didn't ask. I don't know anyone around here anyway. Probably a bunch of high-school guys. They must think scaring chickens is a big joke."

Tad was quiet. He was thinking about the Indian whoops, which made it seem even meaner. "I should have helped too," he said in a low voice.

"Oh, I didn't do much," said Ronnie. "He'll probably still find a few loose chickens in the morning." He stopped and searched suddenly through his pockets. "Hey, I lost my penny."

Tad thrust out his hand. "Here, take mine."

"Thanks!" Ronnie grinned. "Race you back to the tent."

Running made Tad feel better. The harder it was to catch his breath and the more his side ached, the better he felt. I'm going to make up for it somehow, he promised himself. When they flopped inside the tent again, they heard the engine whistle.

"There it goes," said Tad. He knew he'd never hear it again without remembering Choco.

Ronnie suddenly peered into the darkness. "What's that?" he said in a tense voice.

"What's what?"

"Over there." Ronnie nodded toward the alley.

Tad looked at the night shapes all around. Nothing strange, he thought—we're just leery because of those guys. Wait, something did move!

Behind a patch of weeds, tall enough to hide a crouching form, a shadow moved carefully. Tad could barely make it out. His voice was a whisper. "I don't know what it is."

"It's coming toward your place."

Behind the weeds the shape stalked low to the ground, as if on scent. "You ever hear of a prairie cougar?" whispered Ronnie.

"No." Tad kept eyeing the weeds.

"Joe told me 'bout them. I thought he was fooling, but maybe not."

"What did he say about them?"

"Said they were ferocious!"

"Do they come into town?"

"They'd have to be awful hungry."

67

Tad squinted into the darkness. The shadowy form tensed, wary and waiting. "We could go to my room."

"Right!" They scrambled out, stumbling toward the back door. Behind them, the form bolted, too, and bounded across the yard.

The door banged shut and they leaned against it and blew out long sighs. In minutes they were safely asleep in Tad's room.

Mr. Brokaw looked in the next morning. "Have a good time?"

"Sure, except we saw a prairie cougar in the backyard," said Tad.

"A what?"

Ronnie sat up, blinking. His dark hair flared out in all directions. "It was a big enormous ferocious animal," he said.

"Ronnie said maybe it was a prairie cougar."

Mr. Brokaw threw his head back and laughed. "I think I know the one you mean. He's still outside."

Tad raised the window shade. On the neighbor's porch Pinto twitched in his sleep.

Chapter 8

IT WAS Friday when Tad saw Ronnie next. He came to the store with Jefferson. As the pickup stopped, Tad ran out to give the sign for "friend" and Ronnie answered.

"I've got another one for you," said Tad. "Watch this." He jerked his thumb toward himself. Then he held his hand below his right eye, with the second and third fingers extended and forked. Using both hands, he made quick paddling motions. Finally, he raised them above his ears, fingers spread like antlers. He waited for Ronnie to guess.

69

Ronnie cocked his head to one side. "Do it again."

Tad repeated the motions slowly.

"Well," said Ronnie, "you're either going swimming or someone ran over your hat."

Tad slapped his forehead. "I'll do them once more."

Ronnie stared, fascinated. "Boy, you look funny," he said, giggling.

Tad shook his fist, laughing. "What I said was, I saw Joe Running Elk."

"Good thing you told me," said Ronnie. "You'd better let me have the book for a while so I can study it. Where'd you see him?"

"At the gas station. Want to go over there? Maybe he'll talk to us about basketball."

Ronnie nodded. They kicked stones along the sidewalk to the station. Joe was rotating a tire, searching for a leak in it, when they entered the dark service area. He glanced up at them, then turned back to his work.

"Hi, Joe," said Ronnie.

He continued turning the tire and marked it with a piece of chalk before putting it aside. "Hi kid," he said. "You guys want something?"

They glanced at each other, unprepared. "We, uh, came to, uh, buy some peanuts," Tad said finally, trying not to laugh.

Joe pulled a cloth from his back pocket and slowly wiped his hands. "Oh, so this is a business call," he said with a straight face. "I plain forgot," he said to Tad, "that your dad doesn't sell peanuts."

Tad and Ronnie grinned at each other as they followed Joe into the office. "I suppose you big spenders have money for these." He pulled a package loose from the rack.

Tad dug hastily into his pocket. He hadn't thought of money. He came up with three pennies. Ronnie shrugged and grinned.

"Well, now," said Joe, leaning his tall frame against the counter, "isn't this a problem, though." He flipped the peanut bag up and down in his hand. Then he tossed it to Ronnie. "Here. Treat's on me. One basketball player to another."

"Thanks." Ronnie was obviously delighted with the attention.

"Thank you," said Tad.

"That's all right. I've been short myself," said Joe. "Of course, I plan to be pretty well-fixed after this." He thumped a yellow printed advertisement hanging beside the cash register.

Tad had already read the sign. There was one like it in his father's store window:

LITTLE CREEK DAYS OF THE OLD WEST
Games and Rides, Grand Midway,
Carnival Attractions, Raffles.
Rodeo at 2:30 each afternoon.
$25 prizes for Calf roping, Bulldogging,
and Bronc riding.
Anyone Can Enter.
Little Creek Chamber of Commerce. July 3 & 4.

"Twenty-five dollars prize money," said Joe, staring at the sign. He turned back to Ronnie. "Don't say anything about this to Mr. Burdoinne," he said.

"Aren't you going to tell him?"

"No. I don't want to listen to how he's responsible for me this summer." Joe leaned over until he was eye to eye with Ronnie. "He'd better not find out."

Ronnie stepped back. "Okay." He and Tad glanced at each other and retreated from the tiny office.

They ambled back to the store, sharing the peanuts. "I sure would like to go to those Days of the Old West," said Ronnie.

"Me too. I went with my folks a couple years ago."

"There's Jefferson loading the food. Let's ask him if he's going." Ronnie broke into a run. He reached the pickup before Tad. "Are you going down to the Little Creek rodeo?"

Jefferson climbed into the cab. "Haven't given it any thought. Why?"

"Can we ride with you?" asked Ronnie.

Tad grinned and nodded hopefully.

Jefferson looked from one to the other. "Maybe, maybe." He pushed open the other door for Ronnie. "You'll have to ask Prof and you'll have to ask your dad," he said to each of them in turn.

Ronnie scrambled in and waved as they drove away.

"Hi Tad." He turned, surprised to hear his name, and found Bobby Shaw standing in the doorway of the store.

"Bobby!" Tad suddenly realized he hadn't thought much about his best friend lately. "What's doing? You met any of the kids from Little Creek yet?"

"Been helping Dad mostly, but I met one guy named Larry." Bobby frowned. "Who was that you were talking to?"

Bobby's tone made Tad wary. He stepped past him into the store.

"His name's Ronnie White Cloud. He's staying with the Burdoinnes at the school this summer. We've been on picnics and stuff."

Bobby narrowed his eyes. "Is he an Indian?"

73

Tad tensed and looked back evenly. "Yes, he is."

"I thought so. How come you're playing with an Indian?"

"He's fun. We have fun," said Tad, and he could feel his back growing stiff. Bobby was sounding just like Mrs. Dexter, and Tad remembered how his friend had teased Melvin Three Trees.

"He's still an Indian."

"So what?" Tad clenched his fists to show he meant business. "You just better shut up."

"I don't have to. You can't make me. He's dumb."

"He doesn't put snakes in mailboxes. That's dumb!" Tad's voice carried well to the back of the store where Mr. Brokaw and Mr. Shaw stopped talking to look around.

Bobby looked nervously toward his father. Then he shouted. "He's still an Indian. A dirty Indian."

Tad's fist landed with a thud beside Bobby's nose. Bobby reeled backward. His arms flailed out, upsetting a display of potato chips. He tripped and sat on the floor with a crunch. Tad was so shocked at what he'd done that he was shaking all over.

74

"Tad!" His father's voice exploded through the store. He'd be walloped for this sure as not. Bobby held his nose and howled.

Tad's father seized him by the arm and twirled him around sharply. "I've told you never to fight," he said, barking each word. He looked down at Bobby. "You okay?"

Bobby showed no signs of taking it lightly. He yowled again as his father touched the tender spot. "Nothing broken," said Mr. Shaw. "But we could use a cold cloth."

Tad scurried to the sink at the rear of the store and returned with a damp cloth. Bobby looked sullenly at him. Tad knew he would get even the next time they met.

Mr. Shaw picked up the grocery bags. "All the same, Jim, I'd be more choosy about my kid's friends if I were you."

That's the last straw, thought Tad. He glared at Bobby, who looked smug. A small puff showed beneath his eye.

"Tad always has good friends," said his father.

"Doesn't pay to be chummy with Indians," said Mr. Shaw, pushing open the screen door. Bobby gave Tad another hard look and followed his father.

"Tad, I will not have you fighting."

"I'm sorry." He hung his head. A lump swelled in his throat and he burst out, "But I couldn't let him call Ronnie names."

"Do you think hitting Bobby changed his mind? You'll have to find another way to do that." He patted Tad's shoulder as he walked away. "Clean up those potato chips," he added.

Tad slumped onto a chair. His hand throbbed. Imagine, hitting my best friend, he thought. Then he grew angry. Maybe he's not such a good friend, always calling everybody names. And he always overacts if he gets hurt.

Still, we used to have fun, Tad brooded, and Bobby's the same as ever. I didn't get mad before. I just didn't think. Tad rubbed his bruised hand. Well, now he knows how I feel.

Chapter 9

THE DAY of the rodeo was hot and cloudless. By midmorning a haze of dust hung over every road.

"Lots of cars heading for Little Creek," said Tad. He coughed slightly as grit swirled about them in the back of the pickup truck.

"They'll have to put down new gravel," said Ronnie, "to make up for what we're eating."

Tad shifted his position on a spare tire. "I feel like we're riding in a rodeo right now," he said. The pickup jolted around a corner and they could

77

see the county seat straight ahead. Even the town seemed white with dust.

Jefferson stopped the pickup at the corner of Main Street beside a Closed To Traffic sign. The boys jumped over the sides and waved good-bye.

A carnival midway filled the street. They stared in delight at the clutter of tents and carnival rides. Near them a man unpacked feathered dolls and a stack of brightly colored hats. A sign said: The World's Longest Boa Constrictor from the Darkest Jungles. A merry-go-round wheezed out a song, and everywhere there was a clanking of sledgehammers hitting spikes.

"Never saw Little Creek look so good," Tad announced happily. "Come on. Let's get some pop. Then we'll see everything."

They pushed their way into Martin's General Store, crowded with shoppers, and lifted the lid of the soft-drink cooler.

"Let's get orange," said Tad. "It's the best."

"Not me," said Ronnie. "I want root beer." They pulled sweaty bottles from the cooler.

"Drinking it here, boys?" asked the man behind the counter. "I have to charge for the bottles if you take it."

Tad scratched his head. "Could we just drink it outside and then bring them back?"

The clerk flipped off the tops and shoved the

bottles toward the boys. "Okay, but don't forget."

"Take the caps," whispered Ronnie, as they paid for the drinks.

"How come?"

"I'll show you." He led the way outside to a bench. "Take the cork out of the cap," he said, prying one side loose. "All the way out. Then, put the cork inside your shirt and stick the cap over it on the outside, like this." The bottle cap decorated his T-shirt like a silver badge.

Tad fastened his on carefully so the name read straight across. They leaned back to watch the street again, drinking the pop slowly so it would last.

A Ferris wheel creaked through its warm-up runs. Near it, a long tent was open on all sides. The sign above read Ladies Legion Auxiliary. In the middle, women bustled back and forth, filling huge coffee pots, stacking dishes. Fat kettles oozed steam and the delicious scents of onion, barbecue sauce, and hot dogs.

"Sure smells good," said Ronnie. "Hey, you want to sneak into the rodeo grounds so we don't have to pay?"

"I'm game," Tad agreed. They went inside to return the bottles.

The carnival games were opening when the boys came out. "Guess your weight?" asked one attendant. "Pitch a baseball, win a prize," said another. "Here's a couple sharpshooters," grinned a third. "All you gotta do, boys, is hit the ducks."

A fortune wheel spun slowly to a stop at number seven. "You playin' or just lookin'?" asked the man. As they shook their heads, he picked up a comic book and ignored them.

"I'm hungry," said Ronnie, when they had wandered back to the lunch booth. The menu was painted on a sign: Hamburgers, Bar-B-Q Hamburgers, Hot Dogs, Chili, Pop, Coffee.

"I'll have a Bar-B-Q," Tad told the waitress. "And some orange pop."

"Same and a root beer," said Ronnie.

There were only a few persons at the counter as they sat down. Beside Tad was a thin bony man with a pointed nose and an Adam's apple which bobbed up and down as he chewed. Next to him sat a short thick man, who bulged over at the waist. The name Eddie was tooled on his belt buckle.

The waitress brought their burgers on napkins and opened their pop. Each boy added a second bottle cap to his shirt.

An old green car, low-slung at the back, rattled to a stop at the intersection. Doors flew open and people seemed to spill out. Three little boys stopped short, gaping at the carnival, followed by five or six adults laughing and talking among themselves. The driver shouted something after them and the car spun off.

The man named Eddie laughed. "Looka that, Hank. The whole tribe in one automobile."

Hank snorted. "Who's minding the reservation?"

Tad felt numb. He hoped desperately that Ronnie hadn't heard, that he'd been interested in something else. Tad swallowed hard and glanced at him.

Ronnie was staring at the bottle in his hand, but not as if he were really seeing it. He did not look back at Tad, or anywhere else. His mouth was a hard line.

Tad looked around for something to catch Ronnie's attention. Then he saw a familiar figure. "Ronnie, look. There's Joe."

Ronnie did not move, but Tad jumped to his feet. "Over by the store. Let's go talk to him." He grabbed up the last of his burger in his rush to leave the spot. He wanted to move well away from the men.

Ronnie followed slowly, not dodging his way through the crowd as Tad did. Tad shouted, "Hi, Joe."

Joe swung around at the sound of his name and seemed amused to find them. "So," he said, "you two made it to the rodeo." He wore blue-tinged sunglasses under a tan western hat.

Ronnie smiled at last. "You're going to win, aren't you?"

Joe grinned and shrugged. "If the horse is willing. You want a ride out?"

"No," said Tad looking sideways at Ronnie.

"We're going to kind of, uh, sneak in," said Ronnie.

Joe laughed and moved off. "Good luck. Don't wind up in the hoosegow."

At that moment they heard, "Hey, Tad!"

"It's Clifford," said Tad. "He's in my grade at school." He waved back. Suddenly he wondered what Clifford would say about Ronnie. Slowly his arm dropped to his side.

"Whatcha doing?" drawled Clifford. He walked rigidly in new cowboy boots, trying to seem casual. His red-checkered shirt rode starched and new on his shoulders. Tad thought he looked taller. Maybe it was the boots.

"You growing?" he asked.

"Yeah," said Clifford, beaming and rocking back on his heels. "A whole half-inch since school let out." He stopped and looked curiously at Ronnie.

Tad took a step closer to Ronnie and clapped a hand on his shoulder. "This is Ronnie," he said.

He wondered what would happen next.

But Clifford smiled broadly and replied, "Hi ya, Ronnie. You guys going out to the rodeo?"

Tad looked happily from one to the other. "Sure are," he said heartily. "We're sneaking in. Want to come with us?"

"I'm for that," said Clifford, nodding.

"We better get started," said Tad. "The rodeo grounds are a mile from here, out east of town."

Chapter 10

THEY trudged single file at the edge of the road. Passing cars spewed dust in their faces.

Tad wrinkled his sunburned nose and found that it was sore. He glanced behind at Clifford, who was lagging. "Let's wait up," he said to Ronnie.

Clifford's face was a puffy red and he moved stiff-legged, head forward, as if straining uphill. His forehead shone, and a single bead of sweat trembled at the tip of his nose.

"Do your boots hurt?" asked Tad.

"Just a little stiff, 'cause they're new and all." Clifford was breathing hard. He ran a finger around his collar.

"Gosh, Clifford," said Tad. "Your neck is real red. There's a sort of line all around it."

"That shirt's getting ready to choke you." Ronnie grinned. "Why don't you take it off?"

"No, no," said Clifford. "Well, maybe I'll just unbutton the collar." He sighed with relief. "That's better. Let's go."

Tad looked up the road. "The main gate is up there. I think we ought to cut across here. We can go through the fence over by that outhouse."

They waded into the field, knee-high with grass. Tad tugged at his damp T-shirt. Inside his stuffy sneakers, his toes itched. Behind him, Clifford wiped his brow against his shirt sleeve. Currents of hot air pressed at their cheeks. Ahead, Ronnie moved easily, eyes on their goal. No one was paying any attention to the fence line.

"I'll hold the wires. You guys crawl through," said Tad. His foot pressed the bottom barbed wire down to the ground. He lifted the middle wire with both hands, holding it between the barbs. Ronnie and Clifford stooped through, careful not to snag their shirts.

Ronnie held the fence for Tad. Clifford dabbed at his nose and forehead again with his sleeve. He stopped and motioned for the other two to kneel behind him.

"That's the sheriff's car up there by the ticket gate," he whispered.

Tad and Ronnie craned their necks. "Right," said Tad. "Do you think he can see us?"

They looked blankly at one another. "Nah," said Ronnie, trying to sound confident.

"Well," said Clifford, "if we go straight up the rise to the rodeo grounds, he'll see us for sure."

"It's so hot," said Ronnie. "He'd be too hot to come after us."

Tad looked up the small hill leading to the grounds, and then beyond it to where the cars were parked in rows. "We could go around behind the hill," he said. "Come up among the cars."

They nodded in agreement and crept away, taking the long way around. Tad felt the dust burning inside his nostrils.

They made their way through the crowds milling around the grandstand and bought cold pop.

The grandstand was high-backed and white. From a breezeway under the roof, several small boys dropped wads of gum onto the crowd. The ends of the stand were open, covered only by wire mesh.

"Grandstand seats cost," said Tad. "Let's sit on the fence."

"You can see more there anyway," said Ronnie. They circled behind the livestock chutes and the wooden corrals. Calves bawled nervously, and the crowded horses and steers shoved and lunged, spooked by the noise of the crowd. The air smelled sour from animal sweat and manure. Tad took short breaths.

"Those saddles are for bronc riding," said Ronnie, nudging Tad. "They don't have horns like riding saddles." He pointed to several smoothly worn saddles thrown over a chute.

"They don't put them on till the horse is inside the chute," added Ronnie. "That's when they cinch the flank strap, too, so the horse bucks more."

They were opposite the grandstand now, moving beside the high wooden railing fence which rimmed the oval arena. "Boy, that top rail is as crowded as a roost in a chicken coop," groaned Clifford.

Finally, they found space for three and climbed up on the rail to wait for the start.

"It's better up close to the chutes," said Ronnie, looking toward the far end. "All we'll see here are the pickups, or when they drive the animals out."

87

He looked glumly at the catch-pen gate some ten feet from their perch. Once a ride or contest was over the animal would be turned out to the pens. Later the livestock would be loaded onto trucks and carried to other rodeos.

"Aw, it's okay," said Tad with a satisfied smile. He sensed excitement racing around the rail fence.

Clifford rolled the cold, wet pop bottle against his cheeks. He hooked the heels of his boots over the second rail below.

"Ladies and gentlemen. All the folks here in Little Creek bid you welcome to the Days of the Old West rodeo." The announcer's voice barked over the loudspeaker from his small booth over the chutes. A piercing squeal in the microphone cut him short. After several thumps to adjust it he said, "This equipment sounds as balky as a mule going to work." He paused while the crowd chuckled.

Then his voice droned on, "We're going to get underway in about five minutes or so, but first there's a special treat in store for you. Down here in front of the grandstand, William Blue Hawk and a group of dancers from the Flat Rock Reservation will perform some authentic Indian dances. Here they are!"

The dancers moved in a bobbing line into the

arena to form a circle. To the single note of a drum and the high plaintive song of the leader, they moved, twisting and weaving through the dance.

Ordinarily Tad would have enjoyed the dance and found it mysterious, but today he felt awkward with Ronnie sitting beside him. He's probably thinking about that Santee powwow, Tad thought with a sideways glance. Ronnie's face was taut and he seemed to be watching the crowd more than the dancers.

Clifford picked that moment to lean over and ask, "Do you do dances like that?"

Tad winced and Ronnie snapped, "No."

Clifford sat back, frowning. "I just asked."

Tad knew Ronnie would be sorry he'd been gruff. And, sure enough, Ronnie sighed and turned to Clifford. "I do know one dance," he said hesitantly. "I'm just learning it though. And I don't know any others."

Clifford nodded slowly, but he looked uncertain.

Ronnie straightened and then muttered to Tad in a low sad voice. "People always clap for the dancers, but they sure treat them different up on Main Street."

Tad drew back in surprise. He shook his head slowly, wishing he could deny it. His throat tightened, seeing Ronnie so alone and hurt.

Ronnie raised his chin defiantly and looked back into the arena. The dancers were leaving, filing out through a gate at the far end. They seemed to be swallowed up by the corral as the gate closed.

Tad became aware that the announcer was speaking. "Let's start the riding! First off will be calf roping, then bulldogging, and, finally, saddle-bronc riding."

Clifford leaned forward again. "I like the bull-dogging. They have to be real strong to jump off a running horse and wrestle a big steer down."

Ronnie looked interested again. "Broncs are what I like."

Tad hoped to raise Ronnie's spirits. He turned to Clifford, "Ronnie's dad is a rodeo rider."

"No kidding," said Clifford, eyes wide. "Golly!"

Ronnie gave Tad a funny look and said, "Yeah," like he didn't want to talk about it.

"Ladies and gentlemen," said the announcer. "The first roper out of the chute is Ed Smith of Little Creek."

The crowd cheered as first the calf, then the cowboy on horseback, broke into the arena.

"Boy, he's fast," said Clifford, as they watched the lasso sail through the air onto the calf's neck.

The cowboy leaped off the horse, upset the calf, and bound three of its legs together. He raised his arms to signal he had finished.

"His horse really worked good," added Clifford. "You see how he kept backing a little to keep the lariat tight? Wish I had a horse like that."

"You have to train them," said Ronnie. "Ropers use their own horses."

"Thirteen seconds is the time," reported the announcer. "That's mighty good time for anyone to beat."

The boys shook their heads over the next riders, who were slow. One missed roping his calf twice and gave up. Another was disqualified after the calf freed one of the tied legs. None of the remaining ropers beat the thirteen-second top time.

"Now for the bulldogging," said Tad, grinning at Clifford. He added in amazement. "Your face is really red!"

Ronnie looked at the burn spreading over Clifford's face and ears. "Maybe you should find some shade by the grandstand for a while," he told Clifford. "Even your eyeballs are red."

Suddenly, a shout echoed down the railing. A frenzied steer was racing along the fence line, pitching and tossing its horns. Fence-sitters peeled off like dominoes before the angry animal. Tad and Ronnie scrambled backward over the top.

Clifford worked desperately to untangle the heels of his boots from the rail below. He swung his legs high just as the steer gouged his horns into the rail where the boots had been. The impact on the wooden fence jolted Clifford into the air and he sailed backward, slamming down on his back with a thud.

"Are you okay?" Tad knelt to peer anxiously at Clifford.

"You really hit hard," said Ronnie, bending forward.

Clifford's face flushed purple as he struggled to get his wind. He let Tad and Ronnie haul him to his feet and stood gasping and shaken. "That ornery steer came up fast," he finally whispered. He slowly bent to brush off his pants, then tucked in his shirt.

They watched the rest of the bulldogging through the fence until Ronnie announced eagerly, "Now for the bronc riding! When do you suppose Joe'll ride?" They climbed back onto the top rail and settled for the final event.

The announcer began. "Out of chute number two on a horse called Happy Jack is Larry Jeffers of Jonesville. Ride 'em, cowboy!" To loud cheers, the wildly bucking horse lurched from the chute. Up, down, in spastic action. The rider swung his free hand high to balance, but the motion was too abrupt. He twisted sideways and dropped, rolling away from the kicking hooves. "And Happy Jack goes his own sweet way," droned the announcer's voice.

A second rider entered the arena. The horse bucked, landed stiff-legged, and pitched the rider headfirst into the dust. "That's all for number two," blared the loudspeaker. The horse whirled and kicked in violent patterns about the arena.

A gasp swept across the grandstand. The boys leaned forward to watch the horse. The lower part of one back leg was spinning in complete circles from a break in the shank.

Tad wrapped his arms across his stomach, seeing the useless hoof whirling grotesquely, suspended only by hide. The horse whinnied a desperate, shrill cry and tossed its head back, baring its teeth. Pickup riders loosened the flank strap and eased the hobbling animal through a gate to cover behind a rodeo truck.

Clifford pointed to a large man wearing a sheriff's badge. He walked past them and elbowed through the crowd, gathering near the truck. Moments later, a single shot rang out, followed by a jarring, flopping sound. White sand-dust rose in swirls. People moved away, back to the rodeo.

Tad continued to stare toward the truck, feeling strangely cold even in the hot sunlight. "Did they have to do that?"

"Sure," said Ronnie. "Kindest way to put him out of pain. They'd never fix a break like that." He and Clifford turned back to the action in the arena.

Tad's ears rang from the shot. He closed his eyes, and the horse's leg still whirled. He turned and forced himself to watch the next three riders. It was a freak accident, he told himself. But he shuddered.

The announcer blared on. "Now we're going to see a young rider from Spotted Butte. It'll be Joe Running Elk on a horse called Stormy Weather. Coming out of chute number three. Ride 'em, cowboy!"

Ronnie sat straight on the rail. "He's got to stay till the whistle to qualify," he said.

The chute opened and Stormy Weather burst into the arena. The horse reared, ran, stopped, bucked, and gyrated in all directions. It landed stiff-legged, tail high, and head down. Joe tilted back for balance and bounced forward, skating down the horse's neck like a child on a slide. He sat there on the ground with a bewildered expression on his face. It was over.

At the surprising, rag-doll finish, the crowd laughed uproariously. Ronnie stared open-mouthed at Joe, who had risen and was wobbling back to the chutes.

"That's too bad," Tad told Ronnie feebly. "I sure wish he'd stayed on."

Ronnie's voice was low, "He really counted on winning. Boy, that was a dumb way to get bucked off, and with everyone laughing, too."

Tad wondered if Ronnie might be thinking about his father. "Rodeo is plenty tough," he said.

During the rest of the bronc riding, the boys watched quietly. Tad's face burned from the sun; his eyes were sore when he blinked. Clifford squirmed on the rail and rubbed his bruised back. When the final rider landed in the dust, they climbed down.

The crowds outside the arena made it seem even hotter than before. Cars bound for town waited bumper to bumper.

"You'd think we could get a ride, with all these cars," said Clifford looking around.

"I don't see anyone I know right now," said Tad. "Maybe if we start walking someone will see us."

Clifford nodded wearily. Then he brightened and pointed toward an old speckled vehicle, rat-

tling as it edged into the traffic. "There's Jake's pickup!" He ran toward it.

I know I saw that pickup at Clifford's place, Tad thought, but there's something else about it. . . . He didn't know what.

Clifford reached the driver's side and waved at him to stop. Then he turned and motioned with a sweep of his arm and they raced to the back of the pickup.

It began to move before Tad was in. Ronnie grabbed his arm and hauled him up. They sat cross-legged, watching the line of cars behind them.

"This is sure a noisy old truck," said Clifford. "Jake's got the tail pipe held up with a wire, but it's always coming loose."

Tad grinned, and then frowned. There was a strange rattle, like something dragging. He was puzzling over it when Ronnie caught his eye. Suddenly Tad remembered the truck that had pulled away from Choco's in the darkness.

The pickup pulled off the road so cars could pass. Jake burst from the cab and dashed to the rear to wire the tail pipe up off the ground. He glanced at the boys as he finished and looked again at Ronnie.

They rumbled on into town. The boys were quiet; Ronnie stared straight at the road behind him. Tad brooded—could it have been Jake? He does some mean things.

When they stopped, Jake climbed down and leaned one arm against the side of the box. "You picking up some new-type friends?" he asked Clifford.

Clifford looked baffled. "Yeah, I guess you don't know Ronnie." He motioned toward Ronnie and started to climb down.

Jake turned with a funny smile. Tad was stiff with dread. Ronnie's jaw was set and he sat rigidly still.

"You like the ride, chief?" Jake asked, baiting Ronnie. "Say 'thank you' in Indian."

"Hey, what's the big idea?" demanded Clifford.

"Shut up," Jake told him sharply. "Go find the folks."

"I'm staying with these guys," announced Clifford.

"You're going with me," said Jake. He grabbed Clifford's arm and propelled him along the sidewalk. Clifford wriggled and aimed a kick at Jake, which missed. He cast a helpless glance over his shoulder at Tad.

Ronnie jumped down from the pickup and began walking in the opposite direction.

"Wait for me," Tad shouted. He ran to catch up, and then had to walk a step and trot a step to keep up. "We going to a fire?" he puffed.

Ronnie looked silently at him and finally said, "Why don't you go with your friends?"

Tad stopped in his tracks. "Well, Jake's not my friend, if that's who you're talking about. He's plain mean. You saw how he treated Clifford."

Ronnie slowed down and turned back solemnly. "That was the pickup we saw that night."

Tad nodded. "I guess it was."

"I wish I'd hit him," said Ronnie fiercely.

"That wouldn't change him. Besides, he's way too big."

Ronnie kicked at the ground. "Mr. Burdoinne tells me to be proud of the Indians." His voice faltered. "I wish he'd tell it to guys like Jake."

Chapter 11

TAD and Ronnie walked slowly along the midway. Tad was trying to think of a way to cheer up his friend. The carnival was crowded now—a swirl of happy shouts and laughter.

At one of the games a tall girl waited for a young man who was taking his turn with a thick sledgehammer. With comic ritual, he pretended to spit into each of his palms and work them together before seizing the hammer, one hand on the butt of the handle, one midway up it. He raised it high overhead, and Tad gasped at the flex of muscles in the young man's arms. He smashed the hammer's head down onto the base of the machine. A silver ball shot upward to a bell. *Clang!*

The operator grudgingly handed over a Kewpie doll in a hula skirt. The young man presented it to the tall girl with a deep bow that made Tad grin.

"Want to watch this some more?" he asked Ronnie.

Ronnie shrugged, still tight-lipped. Tad walked on, feeling edgy. If Ronnie sulks all night we won't have much fun, he thought. "How about some pop and a box of popcorn?" he suggested. But after buying them, Ronnie ate without seeming to enjoy them. Finally Tad asked, "What do you want to do?"

"Nothing."

Tad scowled. He began to be annoyed. "Look," he said, "just because Jake made a wisecrack, you don't have to be ornery with me." Immediately he wished he'd kept his mouth shut.

Ronnie's jaw tightened. He didn't say anything, but looked angrily away.

Out of the corner of his eye, Tad saw Bobby Shaw approaching. That's all I need, he thought, with Ronnie in the mood to punch someone.

"Hello, Tad." Bobby had his little sister in tow.

101

"Want to go on the Ferris wheel with Sis and me? You can help hold onto her so she doesn't wiggle out." He ignored Ronnie.

Tad wondered if Bobby was trying to square their fight. He hadn't said anything mean exactly, but he'd acted like Ronnie wasn't there. On the other hand, Ronnie wasn't being friendly to Bobby either. Besides, Tad thought, Ronnie's not even talking to me.

"You want to go or not?"

"Sure. You bet," said Tad. "I'll be back," he added, but Ronnie moved away.

Tad bought his ticket. I haven't got enough money for another ride, he thought. I wish I'd waited to go with Ronnie. He wedged himself into the seat. Maybe Ronnie can take a ride alone.

The wheel started up, groaning as it moved. Their chair creaked to the top and stopped, swaying slightly. New passengers were taken on below. Ronnie seemed to have disappeared.

"I can see everything," said Bobby's sister. "Don't make the chair rock!" she shrieked.

"I like to," said Bobby. He rocked forward and back to swing the chair. His sister screamed. Tad's stomach pitched as the wheel dropped forward and started down.

It's always that way, he reminded himself, first round, going down. I feel it inside. But the second round was the same. Bobby rocked the chair all the while and the little girl squealed, "Stop it, Bobby. I'll tell Momma!"

Tad hoped she would. He felt queasy. The man running the wheel shouted at Bobby, "No rocking."

"You didn't help at all." Bobby glared at Tad. "You might as well have stayed with that Indian."

Tad's stomach somersaulted again at that. He ignored Bobby and looked down. Finally, he spied Ronnie standing alone near the penny-toss, jostled and crowded by passersby. I let him down, Tad thought dismally. I'm a great friend.

As he watched, Ronnie drained the last of his pop. The idea of food suddenly made Tad clench his teeth. His stomach rolled desperately. The smell of smoking grease, simmering hot dogs, and cotton candy spiraled up to him. He leaned far to the side. Around and around went the wheel.

Bobby said, "How come you came today with that Indian?"

Bobby's not going to miss a chance, Tad told himself. He was disgusted with Bobby and with himself, but a wave of nausea kept him silent. Better not to open his mouth. The chair slowed to a halt on the platform. He wondered if he'd be able to walk off.

"You coming with us?" asked Bobby.

Tad shook his head. He wanted desperately to sit down, somewhere—anywhere Bobby wasn't.

"I hope you get sick," said Bobby, hauling his little sister away.

Tad closed his eyes, and his head spun. His knees were shaking, so he leaned against the ticket booth.

Ronnie squeezed through the crowd toward him. "Hey, Tad, what's the matter?" He sounded worried. "You don't look too good."

He took Tad's arm and led him from the midway to a sidestreet blocked with parked cars. "Sit down." He pushed Tad gently onto a bumper.

Tad sank down gratefully. He wrapped his arms around his knees and put his head forward, eyes closed. Minutes passed. Gradually the swimming sensation eased away. He smiled weakly at Ronnie. "I guess I'm going to live," he whispered. They stayed quiet, listening to the sounds of the carnival.

Some time later the squawk of a trombone signaled the evening band concert. Tad felt steady again, and they hurried to find seats on the patchy lawn of the courthouse yard.

Tad saw Bobby and his sister in the midst of a small group. Bobby looked sullenly at him and turned away. Tad and Ronnie flopped cross-legged on the opposite side of the yard. Clifford ambled up, grinning, and sat beside them.

Tad hoped Ronnie wouldn't even things with Jake by being angry with Clifford. But Ronnie only said, "What became of your boots?" Tad noticed for the first time that Clifford was barefoot.

"I don't think I'll wear those again until September."

The three of them laughed and then, for no special reason, laughed again.

"What's that light over there?" asked Tad. He pointed to a basement window of the courthouse.

"That's the sheriff's office," said Clifford. "I know because I came up with Dad once to get the hired man out. He was sleeping one off."

"If that sheriff had seen us sneaking in today," Tad told Clifford, "your dad might have had to get you out tonight."

They hooted with laughter and several persons turned, wondering what the joke could be.

Clifford suddenly looked embarrassed and twisted his hands together in his lap. "I'm sorry about what Jake said," he told Ronnie in a low voice.

Tad held his breath. Ronnie looked down at the ground before nodding slowly. "It's not your doing," he said.

105

Tad beamed at both his friends. Clifford and Ronnie, they're okay! And then it occurred to him suddenly—here I've made two good friends in one summer and I didn't think I'd have any.

Clifford's face brightened. "Look," he said, glancing toward the steps, "the band's going to play now."

The band was mostly high-school students, plus a few older local people. They didn't sound as good as a record or the radio, but Tad liked them anyway because this was real live music.

After several songs, the Little Creek mayor welcomed the crowd to the annual Days of the Old West and announced a free movie. As he spoke, two boys unfurled a large white canvas hanging over the steps. It would serve as the screen. Some of the audience wandered away—but Tad, Ronnie, and Clifford were soon laughing at the comedy.

When the movie ended, they rose and stretched their cramped legs. "First my feet and now my legs," moaned Clifford. "I'll never walk again."

"You need exercise," Ronnie teased him. "Come on. You like Indian dances. I'll show you the one that I do know. I guess you guys won't laugh at it."

Clifford rolled his eyes and groaned. "As long

106

as you don't make me dance. With my luck I'd break a leg."

Tad urged Ronnie, "Show us." Then he told Clifford, "Ronnie might dance at a powwow."

At that Ronnie made a face. "What do I need with a powwow? You really have to be good to win a prize. Besides, my dad should be here any day now and we'll be leaving."

Any day now! I didn't know it would be so soon, Tad thought. Sadly he followed Ronnie to the far side of the yard, away from the departing movie audience.

Ronnie broke off a small twig from an over-head branch. "That's gonna be the feather," he explained, dropping it onto the ground. "This is called the Feather Dance."

Slowly he began a rhythmic movement, lean-ing forward slightly from his hips and moving lightly on the balls of his feet. His face was in-tent as he concentrated on the steps, which seemed to cross and crisscross each other. Then he stretched his arms wide and swirled about the twig in great full circles. Suddenly, he swooped low to the ground, as though plunging from a great height. Up he sprang with the twig grasped between his lips.

Tad and Clifford gasped and clapped their

hands, delighted at the unexpected, amazing finish.

"Ronnie, you really should go to that powwow. I bet you'd win easy!" Ronnie just grinned, looking pleased at the praise, and shook his head.

"Would you do it again?" said Clifford. "Just a little bit more. That was something!"

Ronnie made a low, grand bow, grinning all the time. It was quiet in the yard now and his footbeat sounded soft and rushing on the hard ground. The three boys shared the moment of the dance. It made Tad forget his sadness.

He found himself watching Ronnie's face as much as his footsteps this time. For, while his feet followed the remembered patterns, his face was no longer remote or distressed. It showed eagerness and pride instead. It was as though Ronnie had wrapped himself in the spirit of the dance.

In the spattered shadows of the yard, the dancing figure spun as free as a leaf on the wind, whirling this way and that, rising and dipping. This is how it should be for Ronnie, thought Tad —this free.

Chapter 12

TAD slept late the next morning. When he finally awoke he lay with eyes closed, listening to a meadowlark call outside his window. The house was still.

He padded barefoot to the empty kitchen. On the table was a note anchored with an orange. "Good morning, sleepyhead," it read. "We've gone to the store. Help yourself to breakfast." The back door was open and a shaft of sunlight warmed the linoleum floor. Tad peeled the orange slowly. It was fun, somehow grownup, having breakfast alone here. He sectioned the orange, thinking back over the carnival.

He wondered what Ronnie might be doing. Maybe working in his garden. Tad looked out the window. The grass was patchy dry. By August it would all be tan. Maybe I should plant some flowers, he thought. Mom would like flowers and I'd have something to do after Ronnie leaves.

It seemed so close now. Any day, Ronnie said. Yeah, Tad sighed, I'll need a project. A garden might be just the thing. There are seeds at the store.

He ate and dressed quickly. As he left, he pulled the inside door shut behind him to keep the house cool during the day. I'll plant the flowers in the front, he thought—on the east, so they'll be shaded when it's hot.

At Main Street he watched in surprise as a long gray automobile moved slowly out of town. He noticed a small red cross on the side—an ambulance.

He hurried to the store. Parked in front was a car marked Bureau of Indian Affairs. His father was talking with a man wearing a dark blue suit. The man's shirt was open at the collar and he held a dripping bottle of pop.

Tad's father didn't notice him for a moment,

110

but when he did he smiled. "Good morning! Finally decided to get up, did you? This is Mr. Rafaelson from the agency."

Tad nodded shyly at the man, then turned to his father. "I just saw an ambulance going out of town."

"Yes." His father frowned. "Old Choco is ill. Joe Running Elk found him lying beside the road this morning when he came in to work. Mr. Rafaelson was just telling me he's been moved to the county hospital at Little Creek."

His father and Mr. Rafaelson went on talking, but Tad paid no attention. The last time he'd seen Choco, the old man had been silhouetted in the light of his doorway. The memory echoed with fireworks and loud whoops. His cheeks burned when he remembered Ronnie running to help Choco while he stayed behind. Then he thought of something else.

"What about his chickens?" he asked. The men didn't notice, so he said more urgently and in a louder voice, "What about his chickens?"

At that his father looked down, annoyed at the interruption. "What chickens are you talking about?"

"Choco's."

"You mean he has chickens?" asked the

agency man. "I didn't see any."

"He keeps them in that old shed behind his house," said Tad.

The man sighed at this new problem. He stared at the bottle in his hand. "Guess I'll have to go back and turn them out. Maybe they can scratch for themselves."

Tad drew in a quick breath and blurted, "I could go over and feed them every day. I'd have time to do it."

Mr. Rafaelson looked at him in surprise. Tad could feel his father watching him. "Well, that'd be just the ticket," said Mr. Rafaelson. "Would you do that?"

"Sure," Tad said eagerly. "You tell Choco his chickens are okay." He felt a satisfied excitement growing inside him. At least he could help a little.

"Dad, would you still take the eggs and keep the money till Choco comes back?"

His father smiled. "Indeed I will, Tad."

Tad drew himself up. "Maybe I better get over there now and see about them." He hurried out the door toward Choco's house, his garden project forgotten.

Choco's tiny house looked forlorn. Tad wondered if there were two rooms inside or only one. On the south side a tall yellow sunflower grew up to the eaves. It stood with its head turned to the morning light, the petals bright against the weathered wood. The ground around it was cracked and dry.

Behind the house was the chicken coop. A pen area was fenced with chicken wire, which had been nailed onto narrow laths, pounded like posts into the ground. The fence reached the top of Tad's shoulder.

He opened the pen gate, which had a screen-door spring and latch. The coop, too, was fastened with a simple latch and he flipped that open with his finger. The door swung ajar. A musty odor of warm air rushed at him. Inside, the chickens scrambled toward the light, crowding and clucking. Some of them pecked at his blue jeans as they tumbled out into the pen.

A gunnysack hung from a bare nail inside the door. He twisted the sack loose. In it were no more than two cupfuls of corn and something that looked like oats. If this is all, he thought, it won't last long.

The chickens milled about the pen, scratching at weed stalks. There was nowhere to put the feed, so Tad scattered one handful widely over the ground. The chickens pecked at it eagerly. He picked up an old coffee can half full of water.

There was a pump in the yard, and he edged his way through the chickens and out the gate toward it.

He lifted the pump handle and pushed down hard. He almost fell forward as it gave way. Twice more he tried the limp handle.

I'll try priming it, he decided. He raised the handle again and tipped the coffee can to pour the water around the pump shaft, careful not to waste a drop. Then he pumped the handle furiously until his arms and back ached. Finally, deep in the throat of the pump sounded a rasp and gurgle that meant water was coming. He pumped quickly again, feeling the pressure build. After an arm-splitting push, there was a drizzle from the lip of the pump and then a gush. Water spilled out over the wooden base below and onto the dry dusty ground.

Tad straightened his aching shoulders. He caught a few dribbles in his palm and splashed them onto his face. The cool water felt fresh against his cheeks. He pumped again, caught water in his cupped hand, and drank it.

Then he filled the coffee can. First he carried water to the sunflower and poured it around the thick rough stalk. Then he took a full can of water to the chicken pen. He smiled, watching

the chickens dip their beaks into the water and raise their heads to the sky.

I'll pick up the eggs now and come back tonight to lock in the chickens, he thought, as he stooped to enter the coop. Wonder how old Choco manages in here, being as tall as he is. Even inside, Tad bumped his head when he stood straight.

The nests were meager patches of wild grass inside orange crates. Tad gathered up four eggs, holding them between his hand and stomach, but there were too many to carry in his hands alone.

He looked at the gunnysack. They'll fit in there, he decided, and I can bring it back tonight. He worked the sack loose again, gathered all the eggs, and placed them inside the bag carefully.

Once outside the pen, he locked the gate carefully and started back to the store. He was pleased with the job. One day, I may even clean out that coop, he told himself. But first I have to think of where to get more feed.

Chapter 13

TAD swept the small mound of sweeping compound and clutter into the dustpan, then dumped it into a cardboard box. The store's wooden floor was dark with years of wear, and slightly oiled from the compound. Tad liked the way it looked—old and cared for. He was studying it with satisfaction when Clifford and Jake entered the store.

"Lose something, Tad?" teased Clifford. His sunburn had turned to tan in the week since the rodeo. "Or else, what are you doing?"

"Sweeping," said Tad. "I do it twice a week."

117

Jake moved away, leaving them together. "How come you're in town in the middle of the afternoon?" he asked Clifford.

"We're going over to Anderson's with a load of shelled corn. We must be about the only ones around who still have corn in the granary. Everybody's buying from Dad. Anyway, I just came along for the ride."

"Say, Clifford," Tad said, "you suppose I could get a bag of that corn? I can't exactly pay, but maybe I could swap you something." He tried to think of something Clifford might want.

"What you want corn for?" Clifford sounded surprised.

"Oh, I'm taking care of Choco's chickens and I'm out of feed. I've been giving them table scraps, but I figure they'll need some corn pretty soon."

"How come you're feeding those chickens?"

Tad explained that Choco was ill, and Clifford nodded slowly. "Sure. Get a sack and come on out to the truck with me." Tad propped the broom against the counter and grabbed the first paper sack within reach. Clifford was climbing over the side of the grain box when Tad raced through the screen door after him.

He grabbed a bracing wire on the side of the box, stepped onto the rear bumper, and pulled himself up to look over the side.

"Gimme the bag," said Clifford, holding out his hand. "I'll scoop some in."

The door of the store slammed and Tad looked around to find Jake scowling up at the truck.

"What do you guys think you're doing?" he demanded.

It was a good try, thought Tad glumly. I'll never get the feed now.

But Clifford looked over the box as he handed the filled sack to Tad. "I'm getting some corn for Tad," he said in a so-what tone.

"Oh, yeah?" said Jake sarcastically. "What's he plan to do, pop it?"

Tad grasped the bag carefully, stepped back off the bumper and dropped to the street. "No, I'm going to feed it to Choco's chickens," he said flatly.

Jake's mouth dropped open. "What?" He turned furiously to Clifford, who jumped down and stood at Tad's side. "Just who's paying for that corn, I want to know," he said.

"What's the big deal over a sack of corn?" snapped Clifford.

"It's money," yelled Jake.

"Dad won't care," said Clifford.

If Tad hadn't been so amazed at hearing Clifford stand up to Jake, he might have handed over the corn. He stared at them both. Then he knew he couldn't leave it all on Clifford's shoulders.

"You want it back, Clifford?"

"I wouldn't take it back in a million years," Clifford announced in a loud voice, obviously pleased with himself. "I won't even swap you anything for it. It's all yours, and what's more," he paused and looked defiantly at Jake, "next time I'm in town, I'll bring you some more."

"Dad'll have something to say about that," Jake cut in.

"He'll say plenty if he ever finds out that we lose more corn than this on the road, the way you drive," said Clifford, his jaw thrust forward.

Jake angrily pulled open the driver's door.

Clifford winked at Tad. "Be seeing you, Tad. Come on out on the mail again soon, okay?" He stepped up into the cab and smiled proudly as the truck rattled away.

Tad grinned after him, shaking his head in amazement. Clifford finally stood up to Jake, he thought. I wouldn't have believed it. He sure looked tickled with himself! He seems different, now I've gotten to know him. If Bobby hadn't moved, I'd probably still be tagging after him. Tad shook his head glumly. I'm a real follow-the-leader, he thought. Or I was, he promised himself.

Then he had a wonderful thought. Wait till I tell Ronnie. Wait till he hears I got corn for Choco's chickens from Jake. Oh, he'll just hoot. He entered the store and called to his father, "I think I'll ride out and see Ronnie this afternoon."

Mr. Brokaw looked up from a ledger book. "Not today," he replied. "Your mother wants you to help her set up tables at the church this afternoon. The Old Settlers' dinner is Sunday and you know she's in charge of arrangements this year."

Tad nodded silently. Tomorrow'll have to be soon enough, he thought.

The afternoon was busier than Tad expected. "You should have been a sergeant, Mom," he said.

"Six more chairs at that table, Tad. And then, switch that little table around crossways, so there's more room." Tad could already imagine the people jammed into the tiny church basement, chairs back to back against each other, bowls of food being passed hand to hand along the length of the table, and so much talking you couldn't hear what anybody was saying.

At least, he thought, there'll be a few kids around and we can stay outside and have some games.

"How come there's still an Old Settlers' dinner," he asked, "when there aren't any old settlers left?"

His mother laughed. "Oh, it's become a tradition. And traditions bring people together, at least once in a while."

By suppertime, Tad was ravenously hungry. His mother was still reading things off her checklist and describing the decorations to Mr. Brokaw. "That is," she added with a sniff, "if Millie Edwards ever gets them finished." His father was listening to her plans for the dinner, but Tad was paying no attention to anything but the supper before him.

No one noticed a pickup stop in front of their house until Jefferson knocked at the kitchen door.

"Hello, George," said Mr. Brokaw, surprised. "Come on in."

Jefferson nodded briefly and glanced at each of them. He turned his straw hat nervously in his hands. Then he looked directly at Tad. "Is Ronnie here? Have you seen him today?"

Tad shook his head in bewilderment. An uneasy feeling hit his stomach. What's happened? he thought wildly—but he didn't want to know. "I haven't seen him since the rodeo." His voice quavered. "He's not here."

"No," agreed Mr. Brokaw. "What's wrong?"

Jefferson frowned and studied his hat. He peered at Tad again. "He's gone. Most likely, he's run away."

Chapter 14

LATER, in bed, Tad couldn't sleep. Even the rustle of the curtain seemed to whisper "gone . . . run away . . ."

He stared into the darkness of his room as though Ronnie might be hiding there. Why would he run away, Tad wondered. Where could he go? It doesn't make sense for him to leave just before his dad comes. Maybe he's someplace, hurt, and can't get back. But where?

Tad thrashed and rolled in bed. Where would I go, he asked himself, if I were running away? That's silly—why would I run away? And there's really no place to go. Ronnie doesn't even have a bicycle—how far could he get walking? And then Tad had an idea, so simple it had to be right.

Morning seemed as far away as next week. Tad raised the shade to let in the dawn. He wanted to jump up and dress, but he stayed in bed. His folks would want to know why he was up so early and he must first be sure.

Breakfast tasted dry to Tad. He stared through the window and did not hear his mother speak to him.

"Tad? I asked what you wanted to do today. I'm driving out to Mrs. Edwards' this morning with more crepe paper for the decorations. Want to come along?"

He shook his head.

"Be a nice drive," said his father. "Nothing for you to do at the store today." They were looking kindly at him, trying to take his mind off what had happened.

"I'd rather stay here," said Tad, "and read or ride my bike or something." He looked down at his plate, hoping the questions were over.

His parents glanced at each other. "All right," said his father. "If you get bored, come down to the store."

Tad nodded, and they bustled around and out of the house.

He carried a book to the front steps and settled there to wait. When his mother backed the car onto the street she invited him again to come along. But he waved and shook his head.

Tad sat with the book unopened in his lap for several minutes. He shivered in the cool morning breeze and jumped up impatiently. Dad must have opened the store by now. He returned the book to his room, grabbed up a windbreaker and ran to his bicycle.

He pedaled down the street and onto the main gravel road. He did not look back at the town from the hilltop, nor at the school as he passed. His eyes were on the road ahead. At the fork, he turned toward the river.

Morning wind hummed in the tall grass. Above, the leaves of the cottonwoods clattered. He followed the road around the bend leading to the bridge. There he rode slowly across, watching closely for holes that might catch a bicycle tire. The boards rumbled in his ears and the crunch of wheels on the gravel path seemed overly loud.

He looked furtively in all directions as if each tree concealed a renegade. That's sissy, he told himself. But he got off the bike to push it more quietly. Then he stopped and lowered it to the ground just a few steps from the trailer.

Wind billowed and flapped the tattered cover-

125

ing on the windows. The door was closed. It was still.

"Ronnie?" Tad's voice cracked and the wind thinned the word away. He took a deep breath and shouted. "Ronnie? You there?" No answer.

Tad stepped forward slowly, listening. He stopped, hearing a real or imagined thump. Nothing more sounded.

"Ronnie?" What if it's not him, Tad thought. He leaned toward the door. Might be a trapped animal ready to jump out. His hand drew back. Then he was disgusted with himself and pushed the door. It creaked open.

Tad stuck his head into the trailer. It was darker inside, and he blinked quickly before he saw a shadowy form. The figure was crouched on the broken springs. "Ronnie!" Tad sighed in relief.

A somber, thin face was turned silently toward Tad. He moved inside and flopped cross-legged on the floor before Ronnie.

"Gee, everybody's looking for you," said Tad. Ronnie said nothing. "What'd you want to run away for?"

Still no answer. Ronnie's eyes were fixed on a window as if he were studying something miles away. A bobbing twig scratched at the wall outside. The bedsprings creaked under him.

Tad shivered. The trailer smelled musty and damp. He couldn't imagine spending a night here, and he noticed that Ronnie wore only a T-shirt. "You been here all night?"

Ronnie barely nodded.

"Weren't you scared?"

"I heard things," he admitted softly. He looked down at the floor.

Tad rummaged through the pockets of his jacket. He found three sticks of gum and offered them to Ronnie. "Are you hungry? I wish I'd brought a sandwich." I should have thought of that, he fretted to himself.

They sat, working the stiff gum about their mouths. Tad looked up and was surprised to find Ronnie studying him with a small frown. Slowly he straightened up, reached into his back pocket, and drew out a bent postcard. He hesitated, then handed it to Tad.

"You want me to read it?" Tad was puzzled. He flattened one of the corners and looked at the picture side. It was a street scene—a parade of horses and cowboy riders. Along the top, he read: Cody, Wyoming.

Bet it's from his dad, Tad thought, turning the card over to a penciled message: Hi, Ronnie. Got a job with a crew in Utah this fall. You stay with Prof. Sorry not to see you. Dad.

Tad read it again without understanding. "You mean the rodeo is going south?" he asked at last.

He looked up as Ronnie turned away. Tad saw tears brimming at the corners of his eyes.

"Can't you guess?" said Ronnie in a low voice. "He's not with a rodeo. He's on a road crew, moving around . . . same as always. I just," Ronnie faltered, "said he was with a rodeo, because . . ." his voice trailed off.

Tad stared in amazement at Ronnie.

Ronnie's lips trembled as he went on. "I was just kidding about the bronc riding . . . but you thought it was so great that I didn't want to tell you different, 'cause you maybe wouldn't like me. Anyway, I figured with him coming for me so soon it didn't matter." He sucked in a great gulp of air. "He always took me along before. . . ." He swallowed hard. "And it was sort of true . . . what I said . . . he used to ride a long time ago."

Tad finally stammered, "Heck, it doesn't matter. I mean, what he does. I bet he makes good money on a road crew. You never know about a rodeo, I mean whether he'll win or not. And I bet he's real sorry not to see you."

Ronnie clenched his teeth again to hold back the tears and waited to speak. "I'm *gonna* see him. I *am*. I'm gonna hitch a ride." He leaned his head forward against his knees.

Tad frowned and traced small circles on the dusty floor. "It's a long way to Cody," he said. "I bet it's a couple hundred miles or more." Ronnie stayed silent. He did not move. "It'd be hard getting rides, and how would you know where to go when you got there?"

Ronnie's voice sounded muffled. "But I really want to see him."

"Does Mr. Burdoinne know about it, about the postcard?"

Ronnie shook his head. "I carried the mail in from the road. It was on top and I saw it and kept it. He'd be glad about it, though. He always tells my dad I need to go to school.

"I don't want to go to school again, ever. And I'm not going to dance at that powwow," he said angrily.

Tad traced more circles on the floor. "I bet Mr. Burdoinne wouldn't make you do it, if you really don't want to."

"He might. He likes all the traditions and stuff, always talking about the Indian past. What good's it to me?"

Tad scratched his head remembering what his mother had said. "Mom told me traditions bring people together. Maybe that's what he means."

Ronnie didn't seem to be listening, so Tad changed the subject. "Anyway, there's lots else to

129

do this summer. Joe Running Elk can teach you more basketball and we can have all kinds of fun."

Ronnie slumped as if he'd been hit. "Another thing," he said in a whisper. "Joe says when school starts again, you won't have anything to do with me."

Tad gasped. He felt frozen to the floor where he sat. Somewhere in the back of his mind he felt as though he had been caught in a lie. Maybe part of him had wondered about that very thing, but now the answer hit with a fury.

"Joe Running Elk doesn't know a thing!" He spat onto the dusty floor.

Ronnie smiled a little in surprise. He straightened slightly on the springs. "That's what I told him. But—" His words caught in his throat. "I didn't really know."

Tad thought he might cry himself. No wonder Ronnie ran away. He stood up and turned away, so Ronnie wouldn't see his face. The damp trailer made his legs feel heavy and he was tired all through. He ought to be home before his mother returned or she'd be suspicious.

Still he waited, wondering how to help. "I wish you'd come back with me. I'll help you square things with Mr. Burdoinne."

"Don't you tell!" Ronnie glared at him. "I still

might go to Wyoming. There's nothing back there I want." He jerked his head in the direction of the school.

Tad was silent. "I won't tell," he said at last. But he couldn't leave Ronnie like that. "Hey, if they ask me, I'll be contrary. I won't tell them anything straight." He waited to see if Ronnie would smile, but he did not.

Then Tad pulled off his jacket and held it out. "Here, you better put this on. I'll ride fast going home. And I'll come back out soon as I can. I'll bring something to eat. Will you wait?"

Ronnie gazed at the jacket and at Tad. He reached out for it, thrust his arms into it eagerly, and drew the warmth close. He gave a thin smile of thanks. "I'll wait for a while."

Tad walked the bicycle all the way to the main road, because that took longer than riding it. He didn't want to hurry even though he knew he should. When he got home his mother might see by looking at his face that he was hiding something.

He pedaled slowly down the road. Ronnie and I together, we make this ride in no time, he thought. What if he doesn't come back? Really goes away. I'd always wonder about him. Maybe I ought to tell where he is, but I gave him my word.

131

Chapter 15

AS TAD coasted around the corner, he saw a green automobile parked in front of his home. He wondered whose it could be, and then he saw Mr. Burdoinne talking with his mother in the yard.

Tad stopped the bike, wishing he could turn onto another street. But his mother looked up, saw him, and motioned for him to hurry. There was no avoiding it. He pushed the bicycle into the yard.

"Mr. Burdoinne wants to talk to you."

Tad lowered the bicycle to the ground and

stooped to retie a shoelace. It gave him a moment to prepare. I'm gonna have to lie, he thought. His face felt hot already.

"I suppose you know why I'm here," said Mr. Burdoinne. He smiled, but he watched Tad intently. "I am very worried about Ronnie. Have you any idea where he might be?"

Tad's eyes wavered. "No, sir." His voice sounded soft and false, even to himself. His knees trembled. Please, he wished, please don't ask me any more.

Mr. Burdoinne frowned thoughtfully and turned to Tad's mother. "I don't understand why he'd go off now. His father should be here in a week or so. That's all Ronnie has talked about for days. They're very close. His dad usually keeps Ronnie with him, even when he's traveling with road crews. I've tried to talk him into leaving Ronnie here for some permanent schooling. But now, after this . . ."

"I take it you've known his dad for a long time," said Mrs. Brokaw.

Mr. Burdoinne nodded. "Since we were kids. I can remember when he wanted to be a coach and we both had plans to teach on the reservation. But, it didn't work out for him and he was in and out of trouble for a while. Now he's working regularly and I think he's straightened around."

He paused and wearily pushed his glasses higher on his nose. "I have too many kids in school now who think there's no future. I hoped for more than that for Ronnie."

Tad's mother nodded sympathetically. "He's a bright boy," she agreed.

Looking from one to the other and listening, Tad almost blurted out that Ronnie's father wasn't coming and that was the problem. Maybe Mr. Burdoinne really could help—he seemed to care. But I promised Ronnie, Tad thought. He stayed silent, wiping his palms on his blue jeans and shifting from one foot to the other.

Mr. Burdoinne spoke to him again. "If Ronnie isn't back by tonight, I'll have to ask the agency police to look for him."

Tad clasped his hands behind his back to hide their shaking. "Would they take him away?" he whispered.

"If they found him, they'd return him to the school. He'd deserve a good stiff talking to, though. And, if he ran away again . . ." He shrugged and then his shoulders sagged. "You will let me know if you hear anything?" He seemed reluctant to leave.

Tad swallowed a lump in his throat and nodded. As the green car pulled away, he was aware that his mother was studying him.

She fidgeted with the pocket of her dress, smoothing the flap over and over. Finally, she said, "I'm glad Ronnie's your friend. All the same, it's not right to worry the people who care about him."

Tad heard the door close as she stepped into the kitchen. She knows I lied, he thought dismally. She could see it on my face. Her voice had been gentle, but disappointed. Now, he told himself, I've worried her, too.

He dug his shoe into the dust. How can I tell, when I promised Ronnie? Tad couldn't go inside and face his mother just then, so he walked out of the yard and along the street.

His steps dragged and, without choosing it, he found himself walking slowly toward Choco's house. It was the sound of clucking that made him look up.

I forgot to feed those chickens this morning, he thought in alarm. Better do it now. Boy, I'll bet they're hungry. With all that's happened, I even forgot to tell Ronnie about the chickens or Clifford or anything.

He broke into a trot, but stopped short at the pen. The chickens were out, scratching and pecking about. Tad stared at them in bewilderment. I'm sure I put them inside yesterday, he thought. Didn't I lock the door?

He stood puzzling over the chickens until a sound behind him caused him to whirl about. On the warm sunny side of the house, in an old chair pulled close to the sturdy sunflower, sat Choco.

Tad hesitated, unsure what to do, and finally managed a smile.

Slowly Choco pulled himself to his feet, using his walking stick as support. His tall frame seemed to Tad thinner and more pinched together. The old man moved across the yard to the pen, his head bobbing with each short step. He stopped beside Tad, and his face was friendly.

With his free hand Choco motioned toward the chickens. He peered down at Tad. "You took care of my chickens?" he asked.

Tad felt even shyer now than when Choco came to the store. He could only nod silently.

Choco smiled widely then, showing two great front teeth. "Good," he said to Tad. He turned toward his house and gestured with his hand for Tad to follow.

They moved slowly. Once Choco seemed to waver and Tad reached out an arm. Choco rested his hand on Tad's shoulder and they moved to the little house.

At the open door, Choco stepped inside and Tad followed. The house did not seem as small inside as it looked from the outside. Maybe, thought

Tad, it's because there's not much furniture.

He glanced at the narrow cot in the corner, covered with a worn brown blanket. Hanging near it from a nail was the long army winter coat.

In another corner stood a potbellied stove, like the one Tad's father had kept in the back room of the store for so long. Cracked linoleum was on the floor, its edges peeled and black.

Choco seated himself on the bed and searched through a cardboard box, which he had pulled from under the bed. Tad didn't know where to look without seeming to stare, so he glanced around the room.

On one wall, over a small table, there were two pictures. One was a yellowed newspaper clipping, showing a group of boys dressed in Indian regalia. The headline under it read, "Spotted Butte Dancers Perform for Governor." The other was a snapshot of a solemn young man dressed in a soldier's uniform. Tad was looking sideways at them when he heard Choco moving toward him.

Choco seemed pleased that Tad had noticed the pictures. He smiled and pointed to the serious young soldier, then to one of the boys in the clipping. "This boy," he said, "he's my son."

"That's your son?" Tad echoed in amazement. He leaned forward for a better look. Yes, he

137

thought, it's the soldier, only younger. In the old clipping, the boy smiled with excitement and his hair spilled over the headband he wore. Below one knee of his blue jeans was a ring of bells.

"My son," the old man repeated. "A good soldier, you see." His large brown hand shook as he gently touched the picture.

"When he was your size," Choco smiled down at Tad, "he danced like a jackrabbit." He chuckled as if he were seeing it right then. "At night he begged, 'Tell me a grandfather story. Tell me again.'" His voice trailed off as he stood there, like someone lost in the middle of a story. Tad waited for several moments until the old man noticed him again. "I told him the old stories my grandfather told me. They taught him he was brother to all things." His thoughts wandered again as he looked at the picture. "Now there is no one to teach," he mumbled and lapsed into words of Lakota which Tad did not understand.

Waiting there, Tad began to feel as if the cabin had made him invisible, and he wanted to run outside and into the town where he had always lived.

Choco was talking again. "Once my son sent me a letter from the army," he said. "Someone read it to me and I remember it." He chuckled. "Words are all strange on a paper. . . . My son wrote: 'You will teach me more stories and dances. They must be remembered. We are special.' " Choco nodded with a pleased look. "He was proud to be Sioux."

Forgetting his shyness, Tad burst out, "Was he always proud?"

Choco's thin body straightened and his eyes looked away. "No," he replied gruffly. "Sometimes others made him ashamed to be Indian. He wanted to forget the stories and dances." The old man paused and studied Tad. "But my son learned that our grandfathers knew many things which were good. It made him proud." He tapped the picture again. "They sent me a flag to show he was a good soldier. I am proud of that, too."

Then Choco held out his hand, offering something. Tad shyly reached up and Choco put the object in his hands. It made a chinking sound.

"Thank you for the help," said Choco formally.

Tad stared up at the tall man, then down at what he held in his hands—a thin, soft band of leather with rawhide ties at each end and six acorn-size bells sewn onto it. He ran a finger over the smooth leather and touched one of the bells gently—it moved easily, loose on its old thread.

"It's the one in the picture," Tad breathed, not knowing how to say thank you for such a gift.

He smiled helplessly at Choco, looked down at

the bells, and then up again at the old man. Tad thrust out his hand and they shook hands heartily. The old man gave a satisfied sound and nodded.

"Now when we meet," he told Tad, "we can say '*How kola waste.*' It means 'Hello, good friend.' Say '*kola*,' for friend."

"*Kola*," Tad repeated to himself over and over. He no longer wanted to run outside, but Choco looked tired, so Tad left the house. From the road he turned back to see Choco standing in the doorway, nodding a farewell.

Tad half ran, half skipped toward home, thinking all the while of his new possession. He carried it in both hands, hugged against his chest. Imagine, he thought, imagine him giving this to me. I know he's had it for a long time. It's better than any present I've ever had.

And then he had a solemn thought. I shouldn't get anything like this. I was trying to make up for the time Jake and those guys threw firecrackers.

He turned the bell band over and over in his hands, examining the even stitches around the edges. He smiled again in delight and broke into a run, shouting inside. Oh, but I'm glad he did give it to me! Besides, he showed me pictures of

his son and everything. And he called me friend. Wait till I tell Ronnie.

He stopped with a jolt. What can I do about Ronnie, he wondered dismally.

The bells clinked in his hand, and he raised them slowly. He knew what he wanted to do—give them to Ronnie.

Then Tad frowned, touching them, not really wanting to give them away. They're mine, he thought, Choco gave them to me. But they're really more Ronnie's than mine. He earned them helping Choco that night. Besides, I wonder if they could help him feel proud again.

Chapter 16

AT THE kitchen door Tad pressed his nose against the screen and peered inside. "Mom, can I have a picnic lunch? I thought I'd take a bike ride."

"One picnic, coming up," she responded.

He heard cupboard doors being opened and shut, and soon she handed him a large paper bag. "It's already two o'clock," she said. "Be back in time for supper." She did not, for once, tell him to be careful.

The bag was heavy, and as Tad placed it in the

bike basket, he peeked inside. There were two sandwiches, two apples, icy grape juice in a quart jar, and two cups. His ears burned and he hoped she wasn't watching from the window. Then he headed the bicycle out of town, toward the river.

He rode steadily, thinking about what he would say to Ronnie. I sure wish Ronnie had been at Choco's with me, he thought. Maybe he would have understood about learning to be proud.

At the corner, near the road leading to the river, Tad noticed a sunflower rising beside the fence post, another reminder of his visit to Choco's. He turned toward the river.

The bicycle rattled over the bridge. He stopped and whistled softly. No face appeared at the trailer window and he heard no sounds inside.

"Ronnie," he called. "It's me." Still there was no answer. He moved quietly to the door, thrust it open and craned his neck inside. The trailer was empty.

Tad stared in disbelief. Ronnie's gone, he thought with a sinking feeling. He didn't wait after all. Tad was too lost in thought to hear footsteps behind him.

"Boo!"

He twisted around, to find Ronnie, grinning broadly.

"Whew," breathed Tad, rubbing his neck.

"What'd you want to go and scare me like that for?"

"I don't know," Ronnie shrugged. "I was down by the river and you came over the bridge like a ghost might be under it." He grinned again. "What's in the bag?"

"Sandwiches and stuff. It's for you." They settled on the grassy bank, and Ronnie shoved a corner of sandwich into his mouth.

Tad frowned and hesitated, wondering where to begin. "Mr. Burdoinne came to see me."

"You didn't give me away, did you?" Ronnie stopped chewing.

"No." Tad shook his head. "But he said that if you weren't back tonight, he'd have to call in reservation police to look for you."

"So what?" Ronnie glowered at his sandwich.

"You don't want the police looking for you, like a criminal or something, do you?" He leaned toward Ronnie. "You know, Mr. Burdoinne really wants you to stay here for school next year. Wouldn't that be great? We could see some basketball games together and everything."

Ronnie put down his sandwich and watched the water for a moment. "I want to be with my dad. What do I need school for anyway?" This time his voice sounded tired to Tad, as if he didn't mean it quite as much as before.

"Well, so when you grow up," Tad faltered, "you can do whatever you want to."

Ronnie snorted. "Like my dad?"

Tad slowly shook his head. "You'll have to find a different way, I guess. Mr. Burdoinne said your dad wanted to be a coach. Maybe that's what you'll be."

"So I should go back and learn Indian dances, then everything will be great, huh?"

Tad sighed. He didn't think anything he said would make much difference to Ronnie. "All I know is, Choco told me his son was proud to be Sioux. And how the dances and the old stories helped make him proud."

Ronnie looked at him with a puzzled expression. "You been talking to Choco?"

"I fed his chickens," said Tad, "and look what he gave me." He reached into his pocket, drew out the bell band and laid it carefully along the palm and wrist of his other hand so Ronnie could see it all. "It belonged to his son. That Choco," he went on, "a fellow could learn a lot from him, I bet."

He lay back along the bank, raising the bells to where he could watch them and Ronnie at the same time. "If I could speak Lakota," he continued, "I'd really be able to hear some stories."

He paused to let Ronnie ponder that. "Have to do it soon though—Choco's a pretty old man. Those stories won't wait forever."

He rolled onto his side and carefully stretched the bell band out in the grass. "Maybe some other kid from the school who speaks the language would go with me to Choco's and listen to him."

At that, Ronnie frowned. Tad could tell he was curious and a little irked, too, thinking Tad would pal around with someone else. So he added, "After all, you'll be gone out to Wyoming." He studied the trees overhead.

"The basketball team may win the district next year—might even go all the way to the state tournament. It won't matter to you, of course— you'll probably forget about basketball, moving around and all." He paused again, and there was silence except for the soft drone of the wind.

Still Ronnie did not speak. He sat staring at the river, his lower lip stuck out. Finally, he muttered, more to himself than to Tad, "I don't care. What difference does it make what happens on a dumb old reservation? Who cares?"

Tad frowned. "Mr. Burdoinne for one," he began, but Ronnie shrugged that off. The shrug annoyed Tad and he said, "Well, maybe you ought to run away. I saw Clifford stand up for himself

yesterday, but he's probably got more backbone than you have."

"Yeah?" Ronnie glared at Tad.

"Yeah. You're running out on the Burdoinnes and the powwow and Joe Running Elk and me . . . and even Choco, in a way, if it means anything to you."

"Don't nag me," said Ronnie. "You sound just like Prof."

Tad scrambled to his feet. "Well, you'll never be like Prof, that's for sure. It'd be too tough. You'd run away."

Ronnie bounded to his feet, too, and they faced each other, fists clenched.

"A lot you know," yelled Ronnie.

"I know a chicken when I see one."

Ronnie's punch pushed Tad off balance and landed him in the water. He sat up, coughing and spitting sand from his mouth and holding his eye all at once. I always wind up in the river, he thought.

Then he heard the splashing sound of someone walking toward him in the water. Ronnie whispered, "Hey, you okay?"

Tad nodded, hoping it was true. The pain hit his eye again. Not as bad this time, he told himself. He leaned forward and came weaving to his feet. Ronnie grabbed his arm and steered him up the bank.

Tad opened his good eye as he settled at the top of the bank. When he tried to open the hurt one, everything looked speckled.

"Better splash some water on that eye," said Ronnie soberly. "Wait, here's an ice cube from the grape juice." He fished out a cube and gave it to Tad.

"It's not so bad," said Tad, but he gingerly touched the cube to his eyelid. The coldness stung as he rubbed the ice back and forth. Beside him, Ronnie flopped down on the ground again.

Several minutes passed before Tad raised his head and opened the eye. Two Ronnies gazed mournfully back at him. "You're twins," Tad told him, trying to grin.

Ronnie did not smile, however. He looked like the one who'd been hit. "I'm real sorry." His voice was hollow and sad. "I owe you better than that."

"You don't owe me anything," Tad replied. "Except I wish you'd forget about running away."

Ronnie looked away. "I guess I would let a lot of people down. Even my dad. He told me to stay with Prof."

Tad straightened hopefully and asked, "That mean you'll go back?"

Ronnie seemed far away. "I don't know about the powwow though," he said slowly. "I don't have to prove I'm an Indian."

"Heck, Ronnie," Tad burst out, "powwows bring people together. So you remember about your grandfathers."

Ronnie looked at Tad in alarm. "You sure you didn't hit your head when you fell?"

"Sure, I'm sure," said Tad. It didn't matter if Ronnie thought he was crazy. He could learn, the way Choco's son had learned.

"Ronnie, when I came out I wanted to give you these." He held up the band of bells. "I figure they're more yours than mine."

Ronnie gazed at the bells and then at Tad. "You'd give those to me?"

Tad shoved them into Ronnie's hand before he could change his mind and decide to keep them. "It'd make me feel good if you'd take them."

Ronnie turned the band over and over in his hands. "They're real old," he said at last, impressed. "Imagine that."

"You treat those good now," Tad said, fiercely. "Those meant something to Choco."

"I will," Ronnie promised.

Tad rose slowly to his feet and stretched to get the aches out of his legs. His clothes clung to him.

151

Guess they'll dry on the way home, he thought, squirming and pulling them loose where they stuck.

"Look," he said to Ronnie, "if I get home and I'm still wet and my eye is a bunch of colors, it's not going to take anybody long to figure out that I've been with you. So, now, are you coming back with me or not?" He held his breath.

Ronnie was still turning the band in his hands. He glanced up and slowly shook his head.

Tad felt a familiar lump in his throat. He'd been so sure. Now, there was nothing more he could say.

Ronnie must have noticed the slump in Tad's shoulders, because he smiled gently. "I want to sit here and think about things. Maybe I will go back after a while." He grinned like the old Ronnie. "At least before they get out the scouts." Then his face sobered again, "But I sure wanted to see my dad. I could still try hitching rides."

Tad turned away and walked up the riverbank to his bicycle. He looked back at Ronnie, who was staring at the river.

At the main road Tad climbed onto the bike. His head ached, and so did his back and legs. While he pedaled he thought of Mr. Burdoinne's worried face as he spoke of his students. And of Choco's sad face speaking of the son who would

never again know pride in the Sioux. And he
wondered about Ronnie's father—far away and
probably lonesome.

If Ronnie's not back in the morning, Tad decided grimly, I'll call Mr. Burdoinne. Right now,
it's up to Ronnie.

Chapter 17

THE following morning, Mr. Burdoinne called the store. "Ronnie's back," he told Tad's father. "I'm giving him some special work projects this week."

"What's that supposed to mean?" Tad asked his father suspiciously.

"It means that Ronnie's not going to be able to play this week," his father said. "He's being disciplined. You'd better find some projects of your own to fill the time."

And so, to keep from wondering about Ronnie, Tad pestered everyone for jobs that would keep him busy. He gave the bench in front of the store a fresh coat of green paint. He volunteered to feed Pinto for three days while his owners were gone—and tried not to mind that the dog snarled at him each time.

One morning his moccasin kit arrived in the mail. He carried it home and spent two days putting them together—lacing them carefully and sewing the red, white, and blue eagle emblems on perfectly straight.

When he put the moccasins on he was pleased that they fit well. Of course, he had to admit, they're not like the bell band—they're not the real McCoy. But neither am I, he thought, laughing at himself. More than anything they made him think, not of the ancient Indians, but of Ronnie.

This week will never be over, he thought. I wonder what Ronnie's doing. I wonder if he'll be staying. There's plenty of summer left for fun, unless he has too much to do.

One afternoon he carried a pail of water into the back yard and washed his bicycle carefully. When he was through he rubbed on a thin coat of wax and then polished it to make it shine. Just like new, he thought, pleased with his work. Guess I'll ride down and show Dad.

He pedaled slowly to avoid getting dust on his

shining bike. As he rounded the corner near the filling station he could see someone seated on the long bench by the store. It was Ronnie.

He raced to the store, shouting, "Ronnie! Hi!"

Ronnie grinned back at him. "Hi! You got a new bike?"

"Nope. I got busy and washed it." They smiled happily at each other. Tad leaned the bicycle against the store and noticed that the school pickup was backed in at the curb. "You come in with Jefferson?"

Ronnie nodded. "Yeah, I have to go back with him, too. I'm pulling weeds this afternoon and I'm not done. Mr. Burdoinne says the zinnia crop better be good." They giggled, and Tad sat down beside Ronnie.

"They've really been keeping you busy, I guess," Tad said.

"Wow. You wouldn't believe they could think of so much. I bet I haven't shot but five baskets all week." He shook his head, grinning as he did, "I even helped Mrs. Burdoinne in the school library. Can you see that? She's fixing some torn books—gluing on new bindings and putting them in presses and like that. Boy, my fingers have been glued together all week."

They laughed. Ronnie seemed to be taking everything in good spirits. Tad had many questions, but he didn't want to pry, so he let Ronnie talk about whatever he wanted to.

Ronnie looked down thoughtfully and then spoke. "You know what Prof did? He called out to Wyoming and let me talk to my dad, right on the telephone. It was just like he was in the next room. I never did that before." Ronnie seemed pleased, just remembering the call.

"Did he know about you?" Tad asked. "What did he say?"

"Yeah, I told him. He sort of chewed me out and told me not to do it again. And said stuff about how Prof was right and I should learn about all the old things and all the new things, too, so I could amount to something. Boy, he sounded just like Prof for a while."

"You're staying then?"

Ronnie nodded. "He said when school's out next spring maybe I could come down and see him. You know, ride the bus or something. I don't know though."

"Sounds like fun," Tad put in before Ronnie could start worrying about it.

Jefferson came from the store with a box of groceries. "Hi, boys," he said. "You two waiting for one of them prairie cougars to come down Main Street?"

They glanced sideways at each other, drew in

their chins, and stayed silent. Jefferson chuckled as he put the box in the pickup.

"I'm going to mail some letters, Ronnie. You be ready to go when I get back."

They watched the stocky man cross the street to the post office.

Ronnie sighed, "Guess I'll have to go. Mr. Burdoinne said when I get the weeding done and maybe help some more on the books, I can come in and see you again."

"That's great," said Tad.

"And the following weekend, I can ask you if you want to come with us to Santee." His mouth tightened a bit at the corners when he said it.

"No kidding. You going to be in one of the powwow contests?"

Ronnie nodded without much enthusiasm. "That feather dance. Joe Running Elk keeps saying, isn't it too bad some bird is being done out of a feather just for me. Boy, high-school guys think they're so smart."

Tad shook his head in sympathy and Ronnie brightened.

"Mrs. Burdoinne took an old leather jacket of Prof's and cut it up to make me a vest to wear in the dance. She put some beads on it even. And you know what else?" Ronnie was grinning widely now.

"Remember the lucky penny? Well, I drilled a hole in it, and she sewed it right into the design on the vest."

"Neat," said Tad in admiration. "Sounds neat."

"Well, the best part is," Ronnie went on, "that bell band. I bet nobody will have anything better than that." He looked directly at Tad. "I really like those bells and, you know, we can share them. You can wear them sometime, if you want."

Ronnie seemed so full of plans Tad might have envied him if he hadn't been so happy for him.

Jefferson came back from the post office and climbed up into the pickup. "Pick your seat," he told Ronnie.

Ronnie hopped onto the back of the pickup, his legs dangling over the end where the tailgate was down. He brushed a lock of dark hair back from his brow as the pickup jolted away from the curb.

Tad watched him inch his way backward until he was leaning against the back of the cab. As the pickup took the corner, a cloud of dust hung in the warm, still air. The two boys raised their arms in greeting.

HARPER TROPHY BOOKS

you will enjoy reading

HARPER & ROW, PUBLISHERS, INC.
10 East 53rd Street, New York, New York 10022